HUE COLORING

Tattoo Coloring Book

IN THIS COLORING BOOK...
50 Tattoo Coloring Designs are included in this adult coloring book to help you relax and make your life more colorful. These illustrations are created for you to bring enjoyment to your life, and designed with beautiful patterns that appeal to adult eyes.

TIPS TO A FUN COLORING
Find a quiet space. It's easier to focus on what you are doing when there are no distractions.

Organize your materials. Lay out your coloring book and crayons, pens, or pencils.

Set the mood. Turn on some tranquil music, diffuse lavender or another relaxing oil, and make sure you have your preferred drink at hand.

Select your picture. Which image speaks to you today? That's the one you should color. Choose your palette. Select the colors you will be using for your image.

Begin coloring. This is the fun part. Don't worry about getting everything perfect; just start. If you feel you don't want to do it anymore, just stop!

SHOW US YOUR CREATION!
We'd love to hear from you, show us what you created.
Facebook: www.facebook.com/huecoloring
Pinterest: www.pinterest.com/huecoloring
Please be sure to subscribe to our newsletter by visiting: huecoloring.com. We'll show you our latest coloring projects as well as giving you information of the best deals.

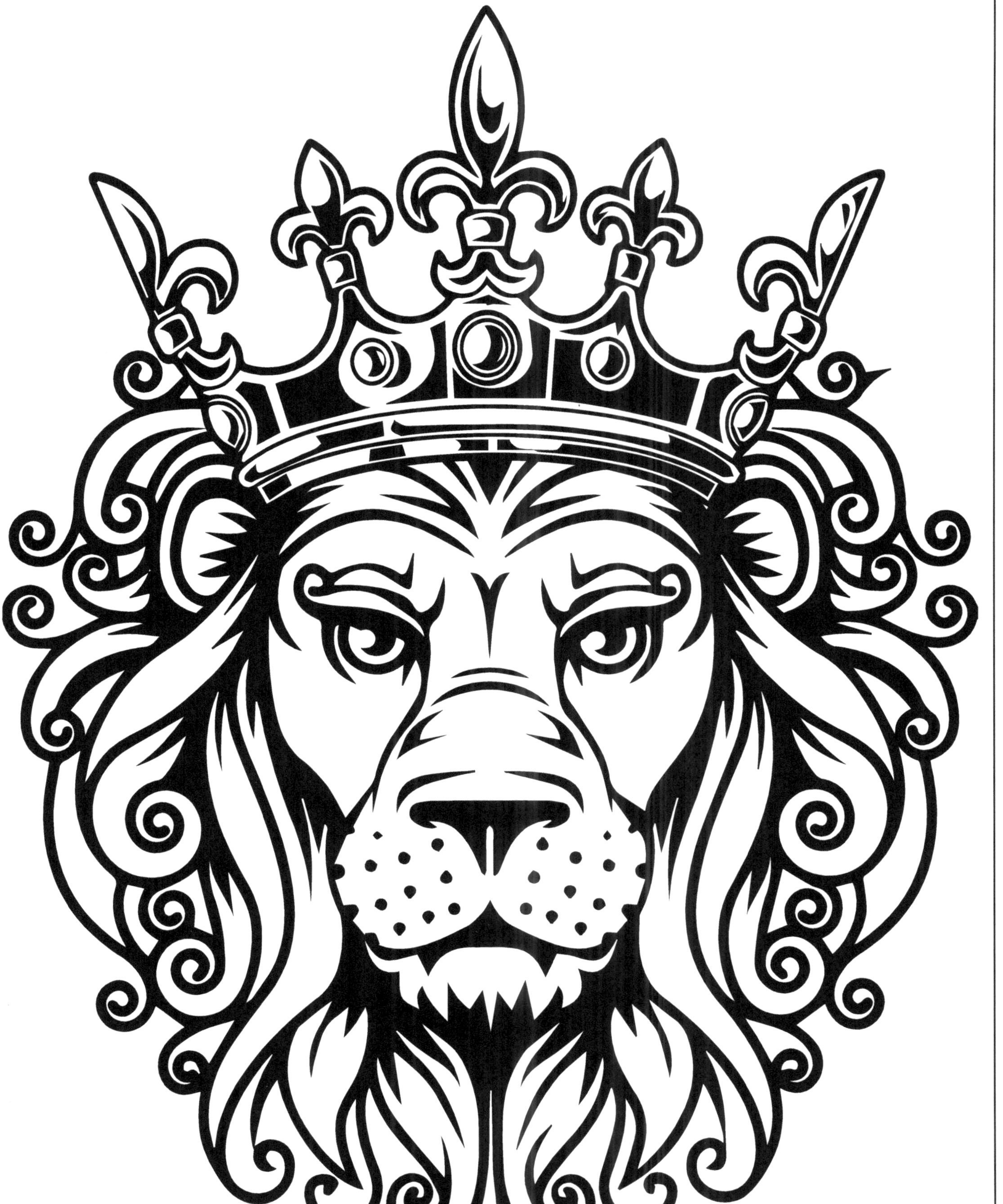

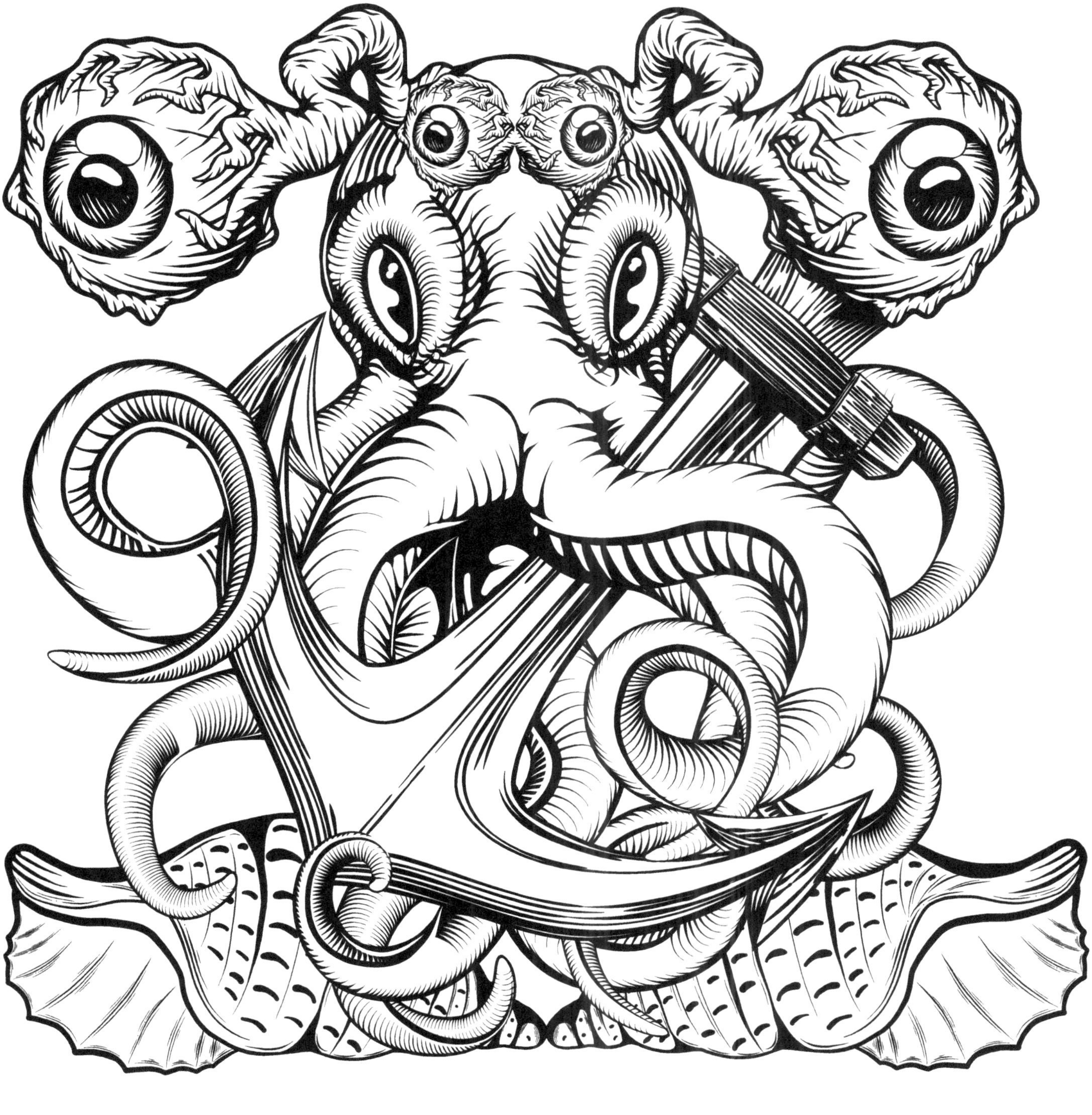

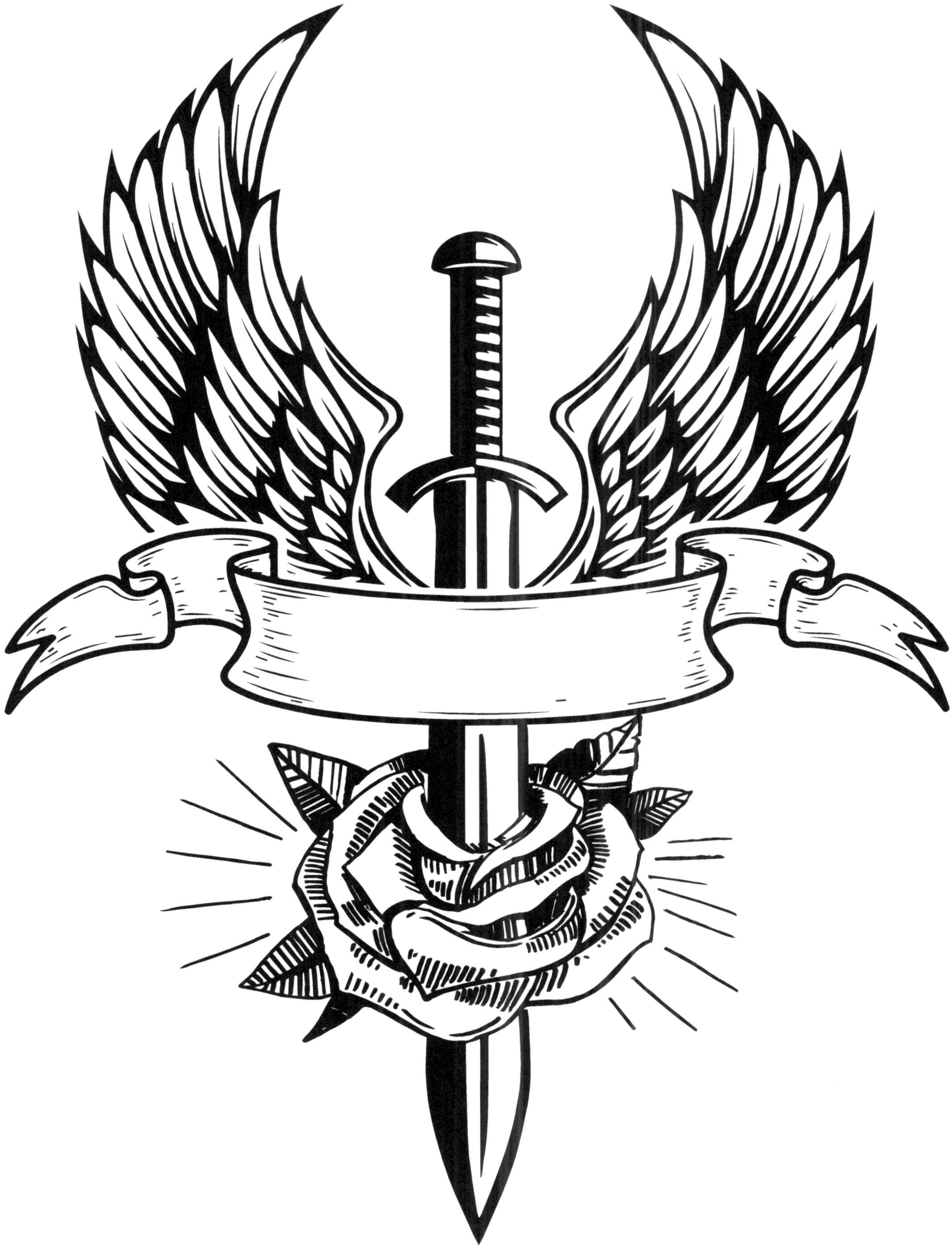

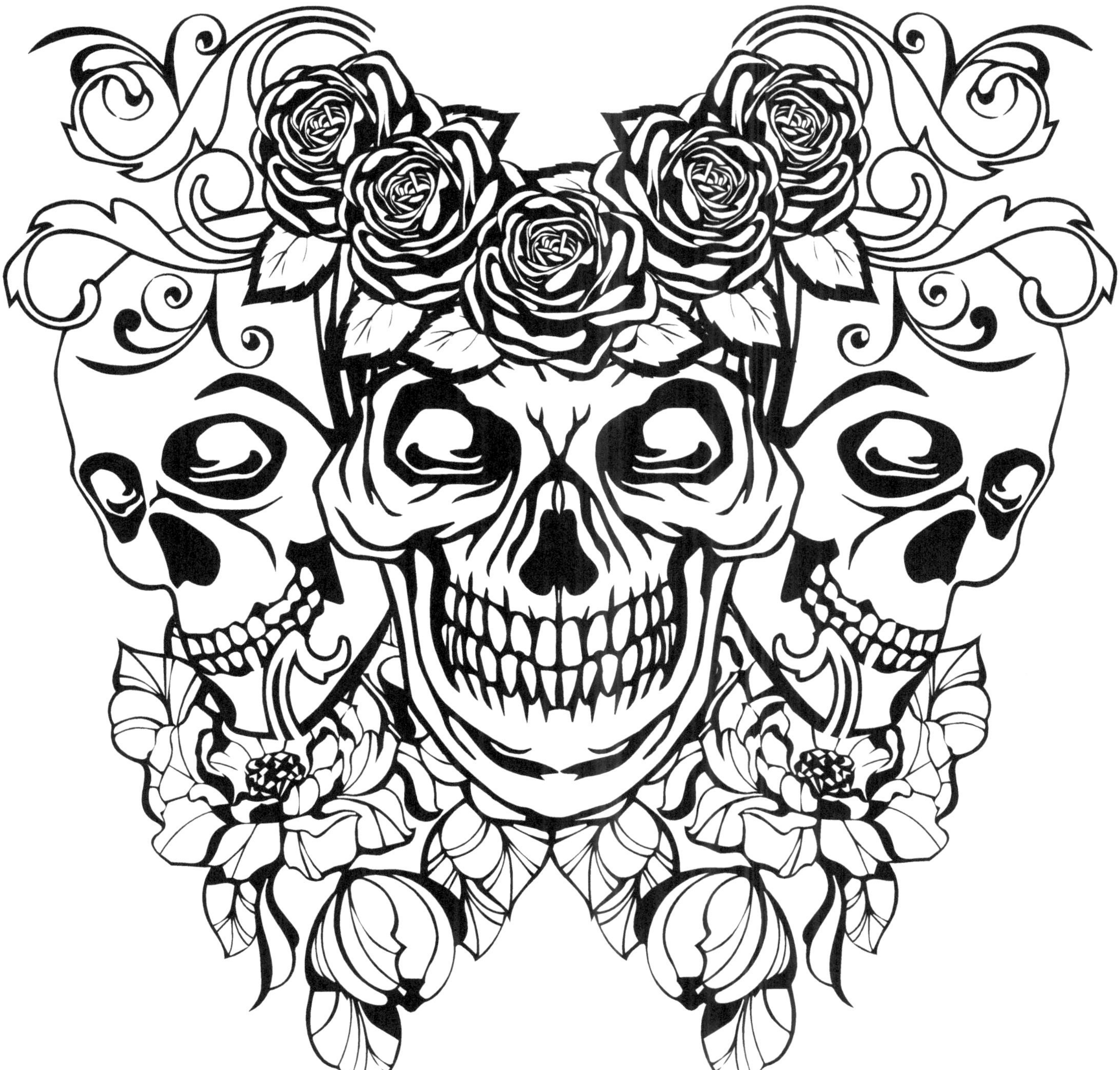

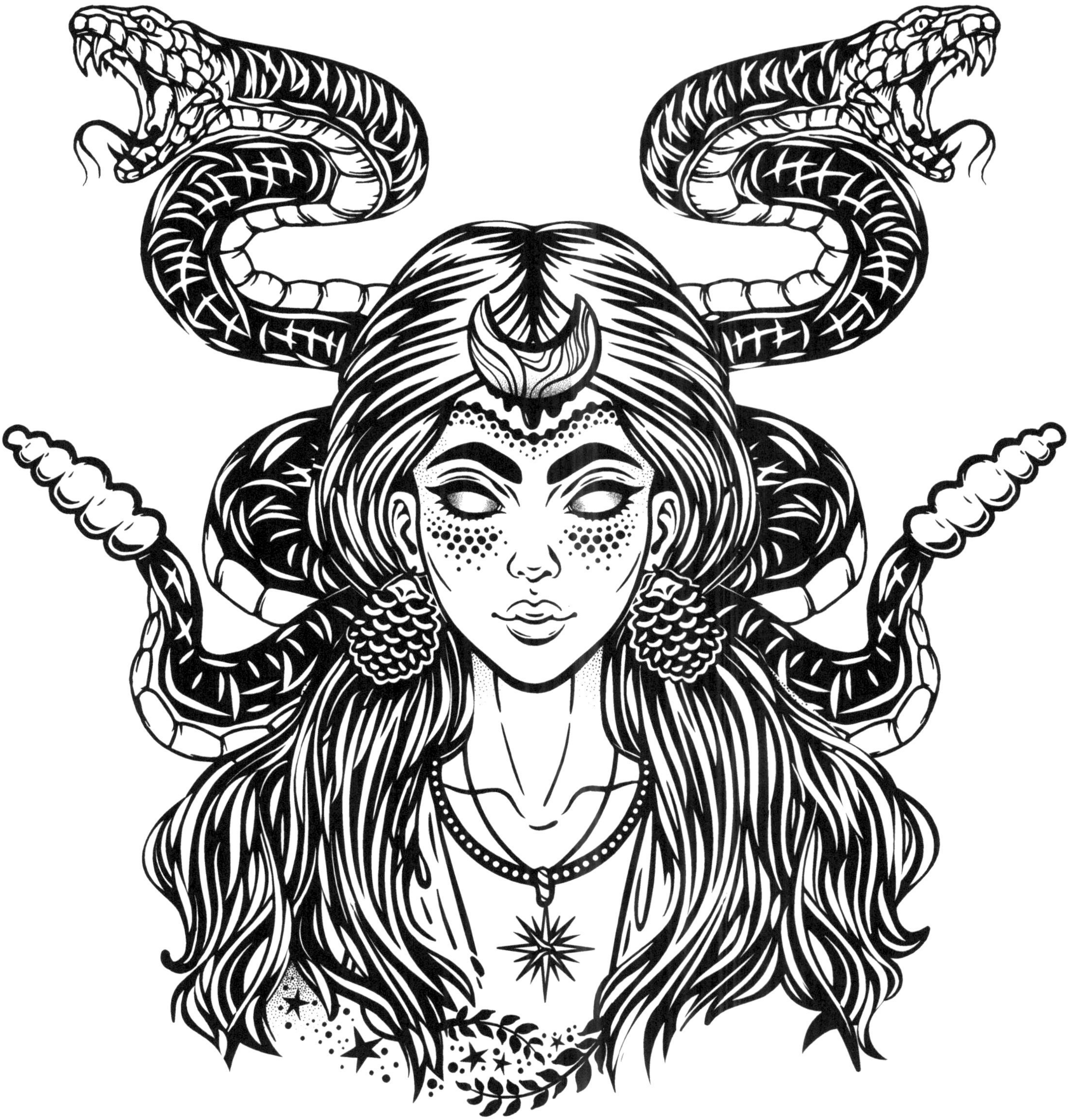

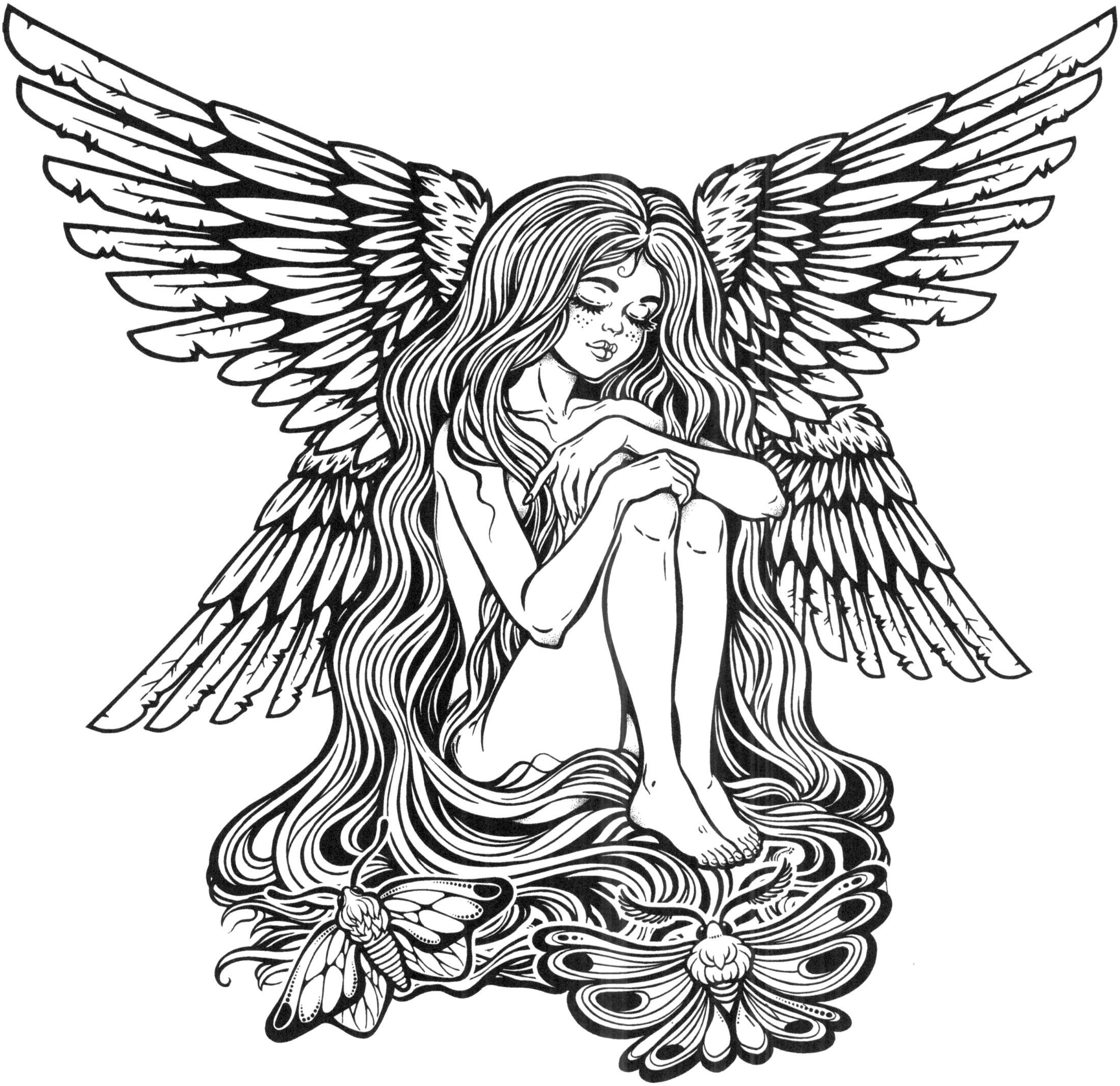

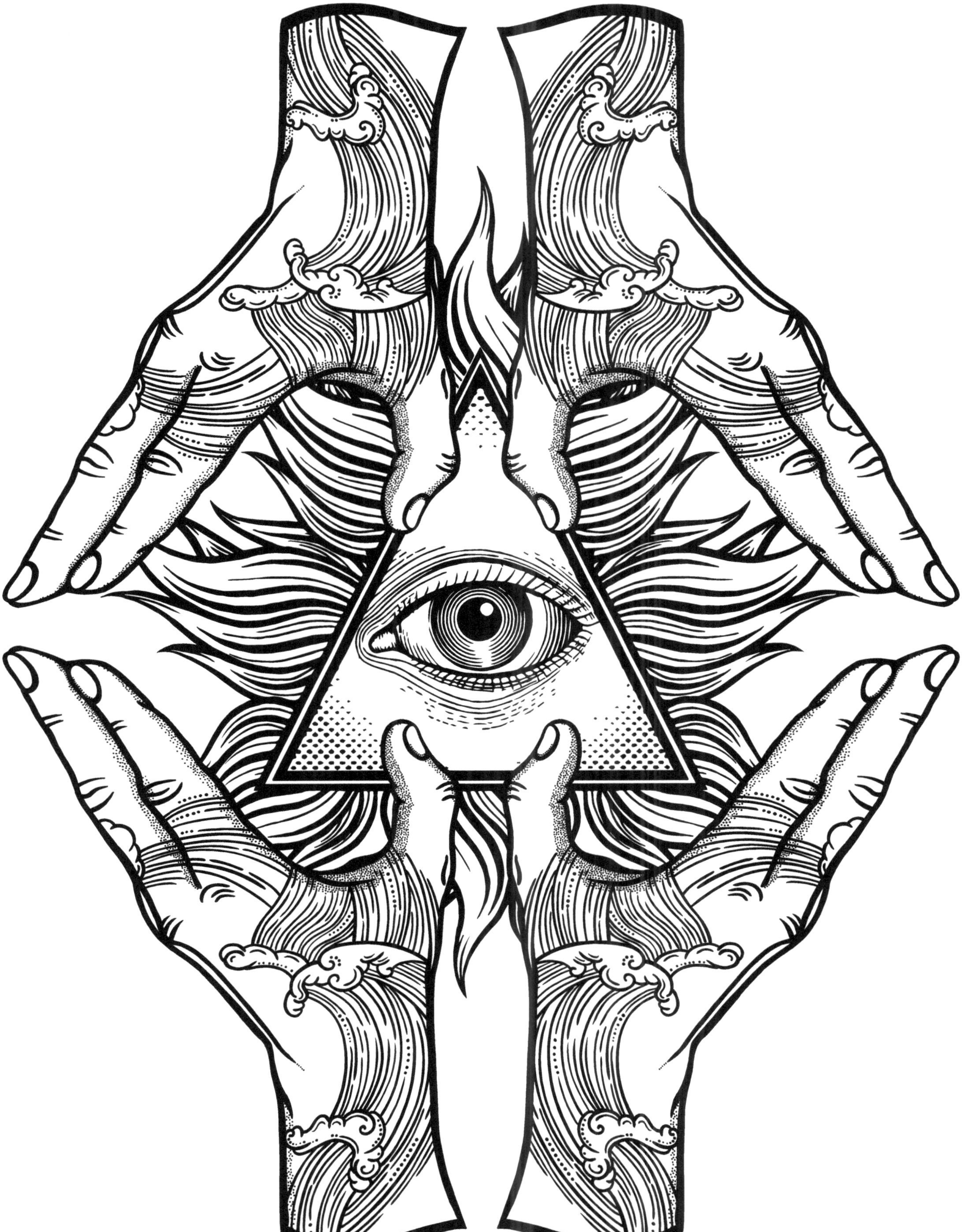

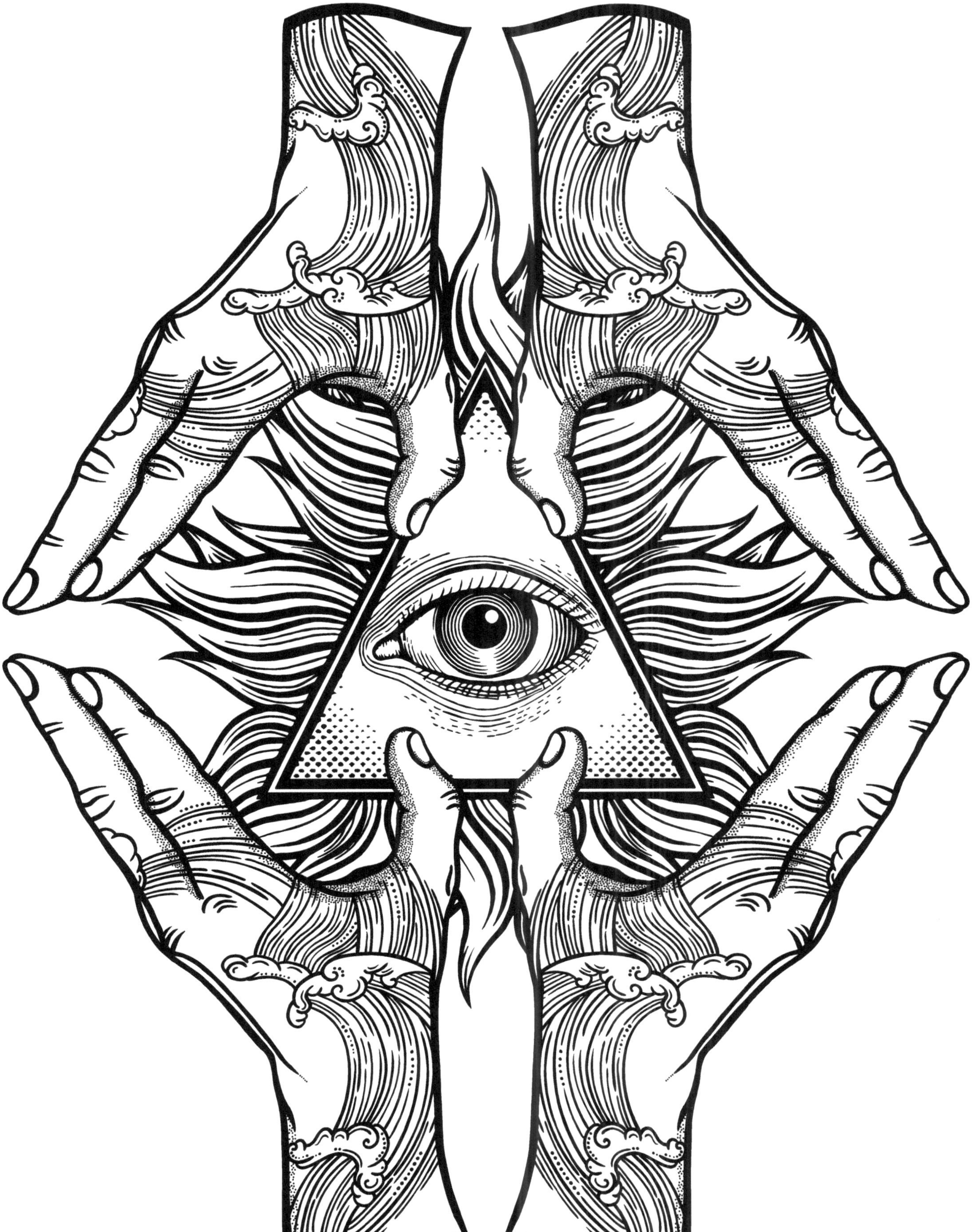

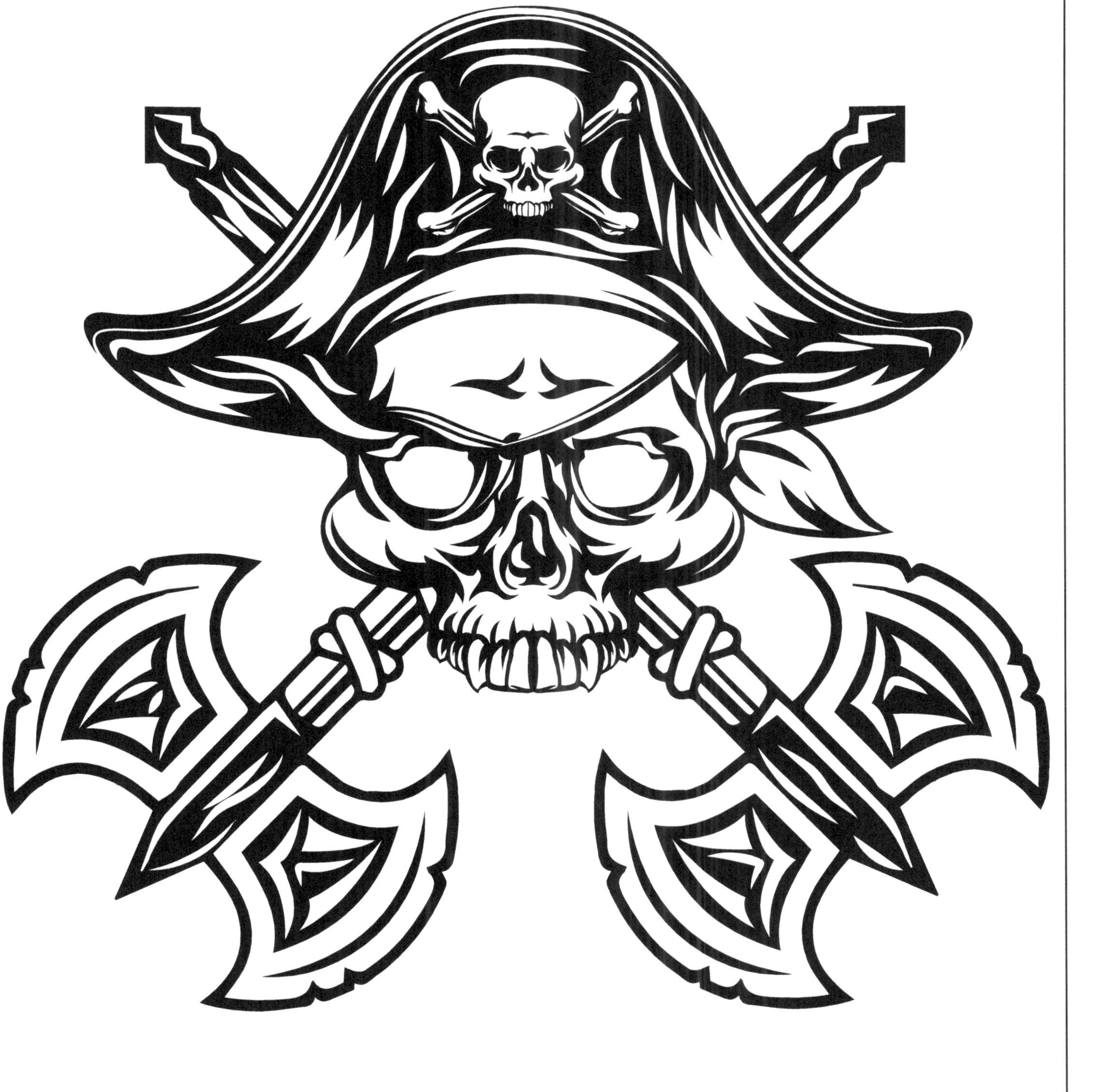

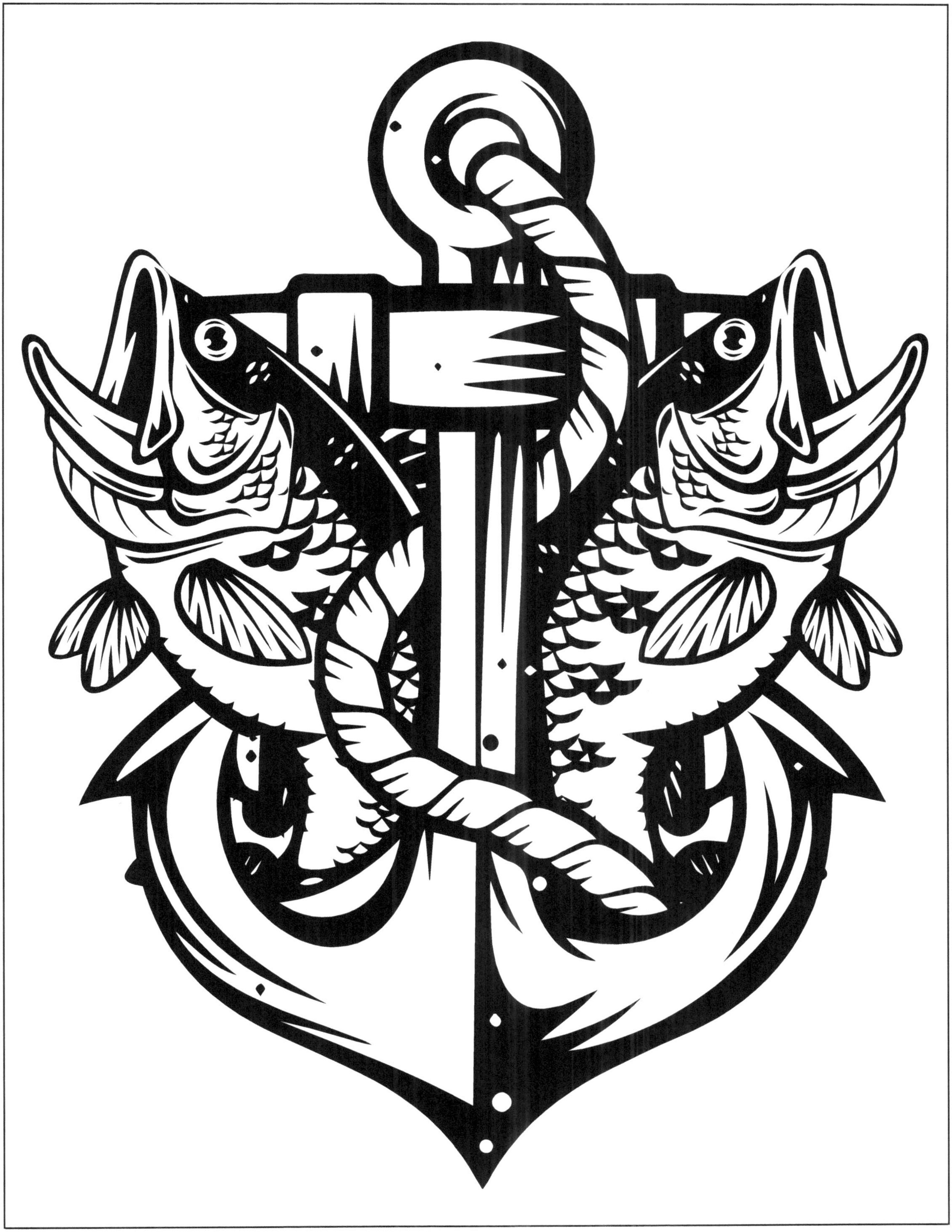

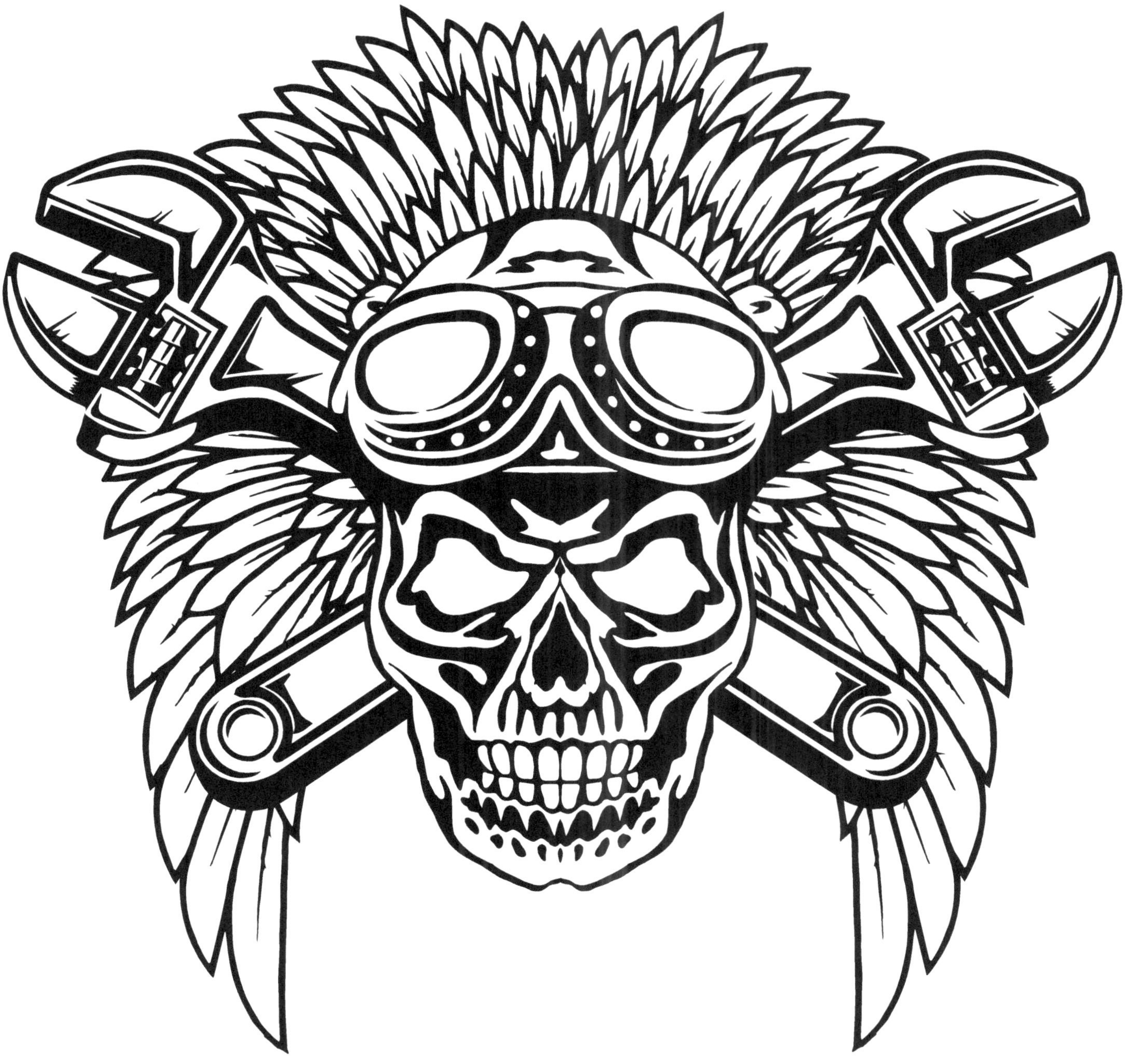

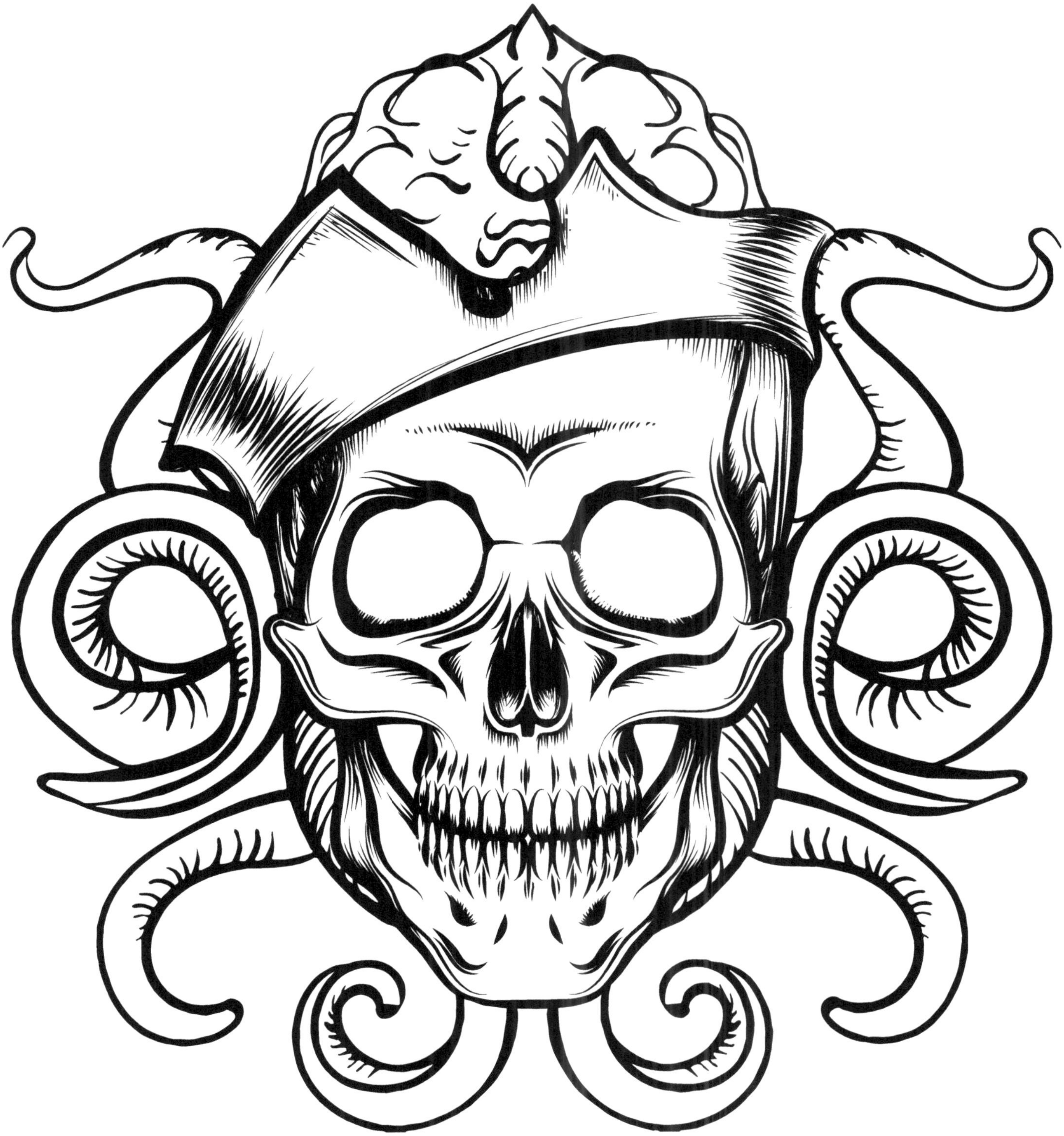

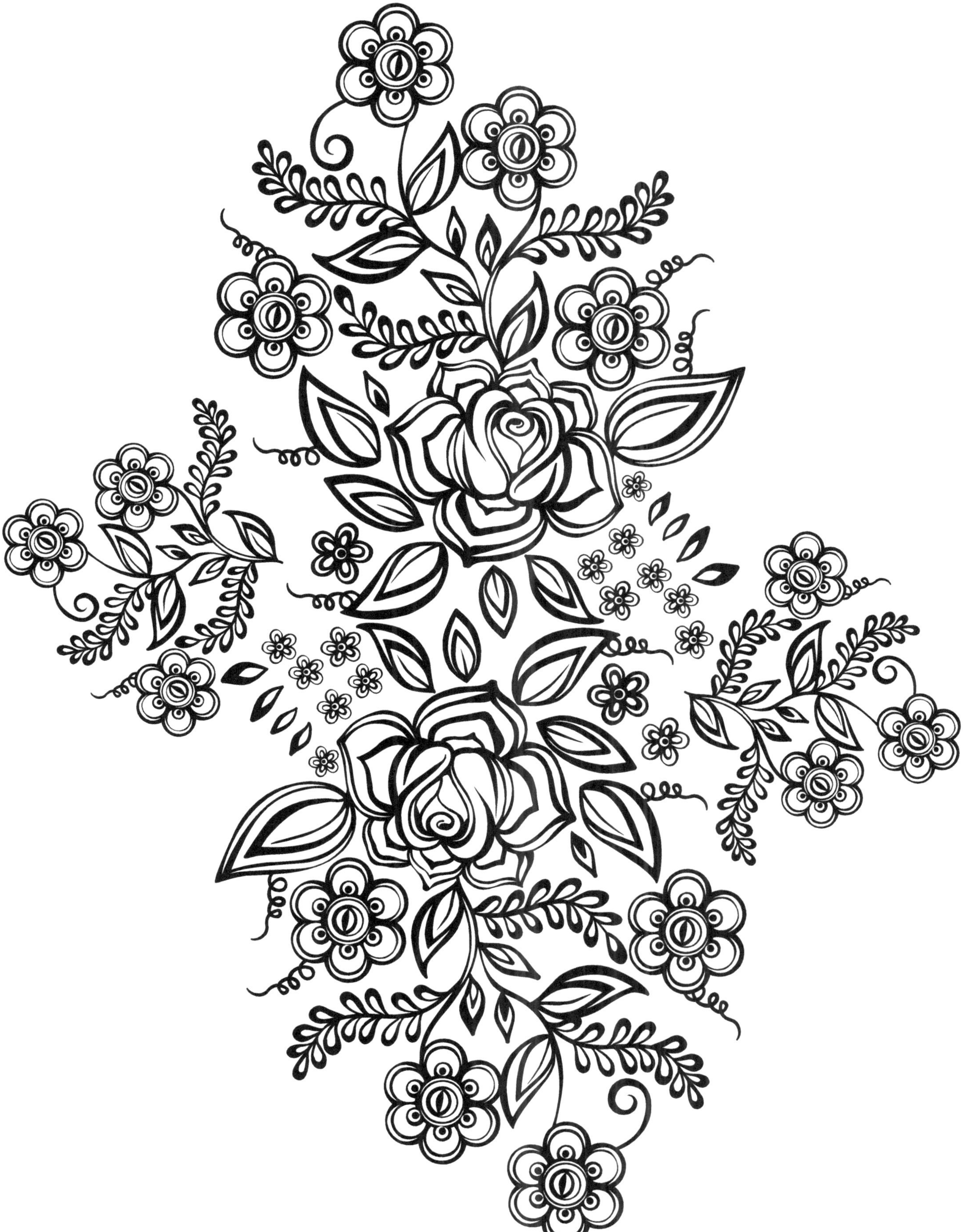

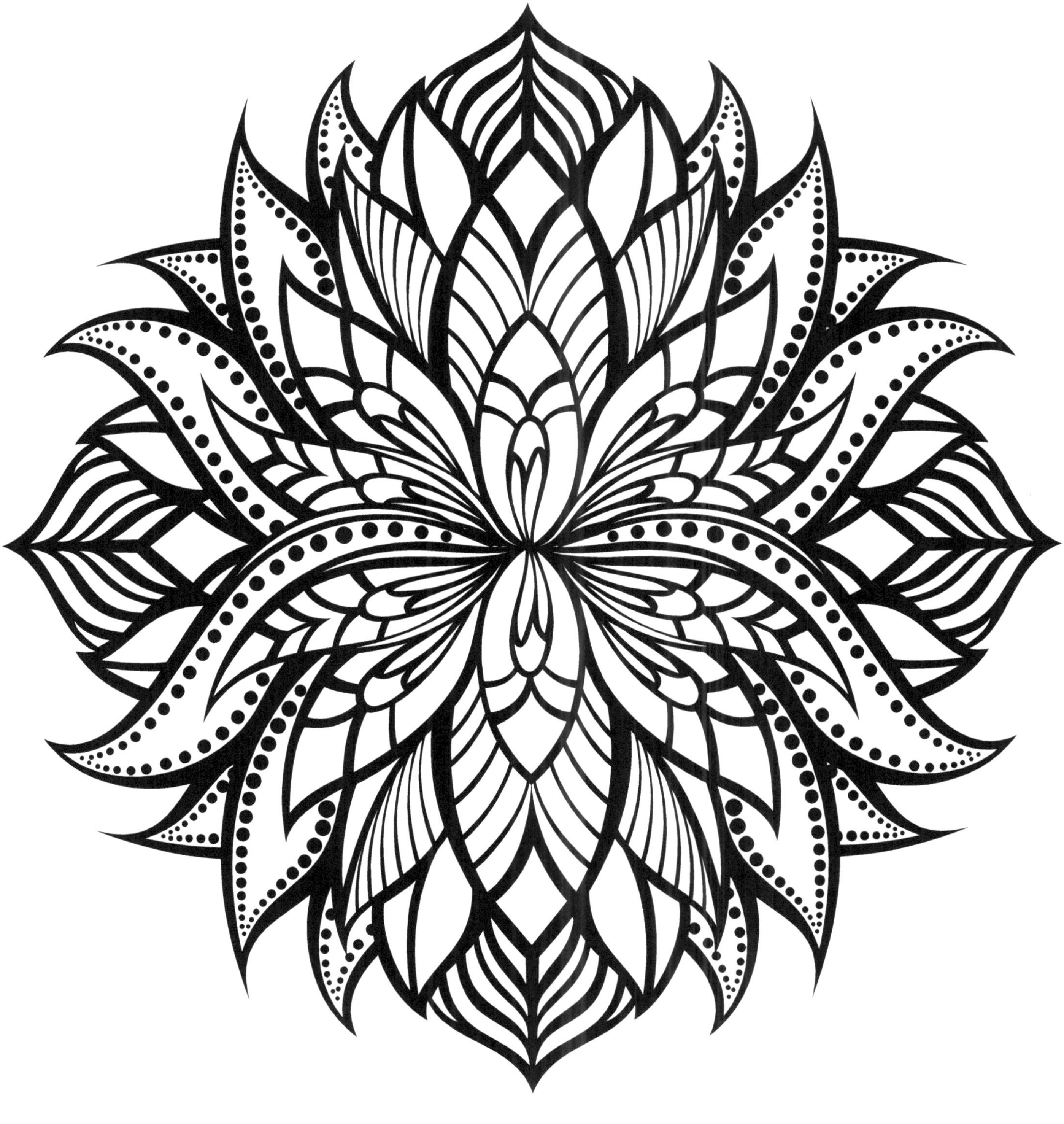

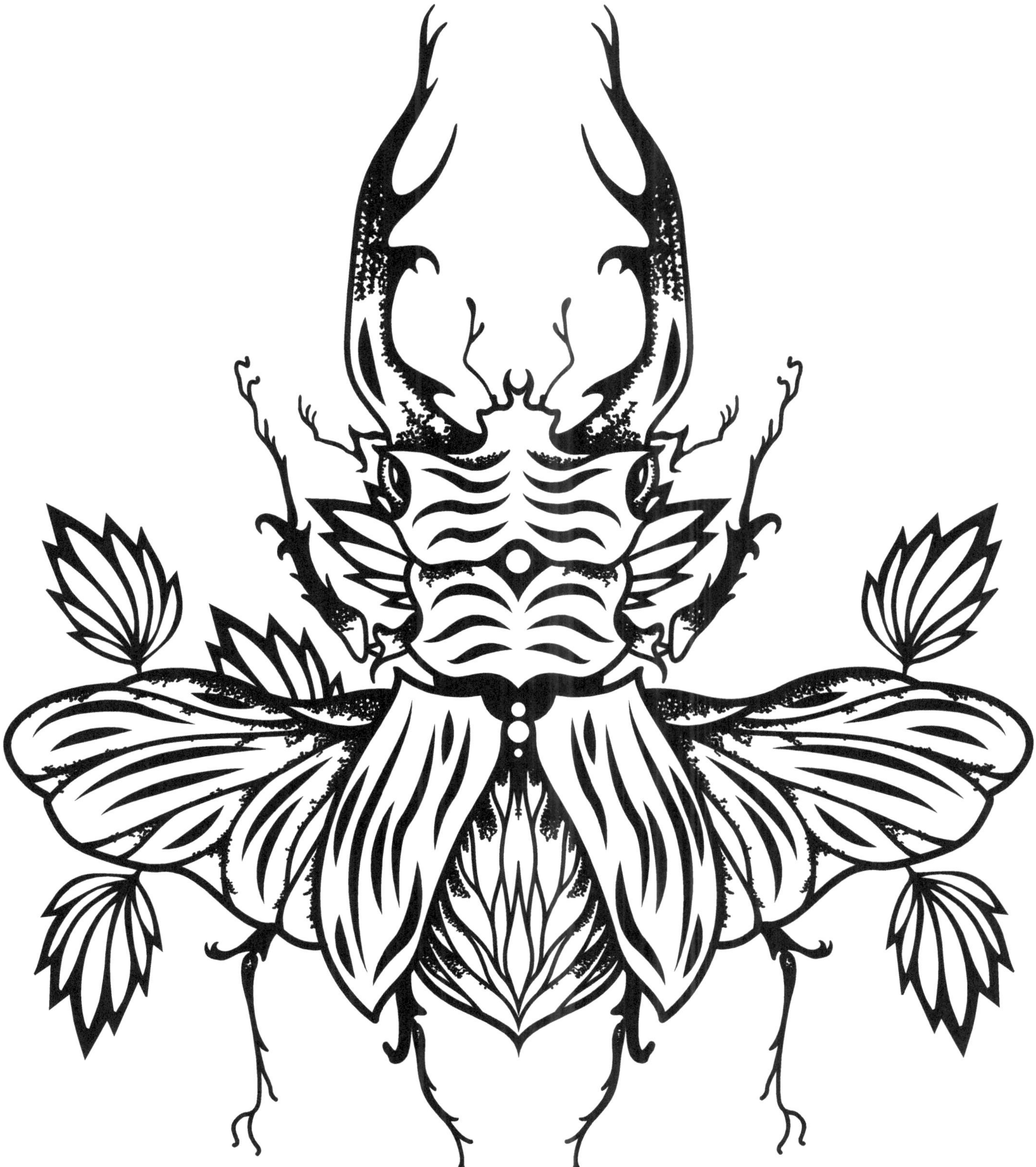

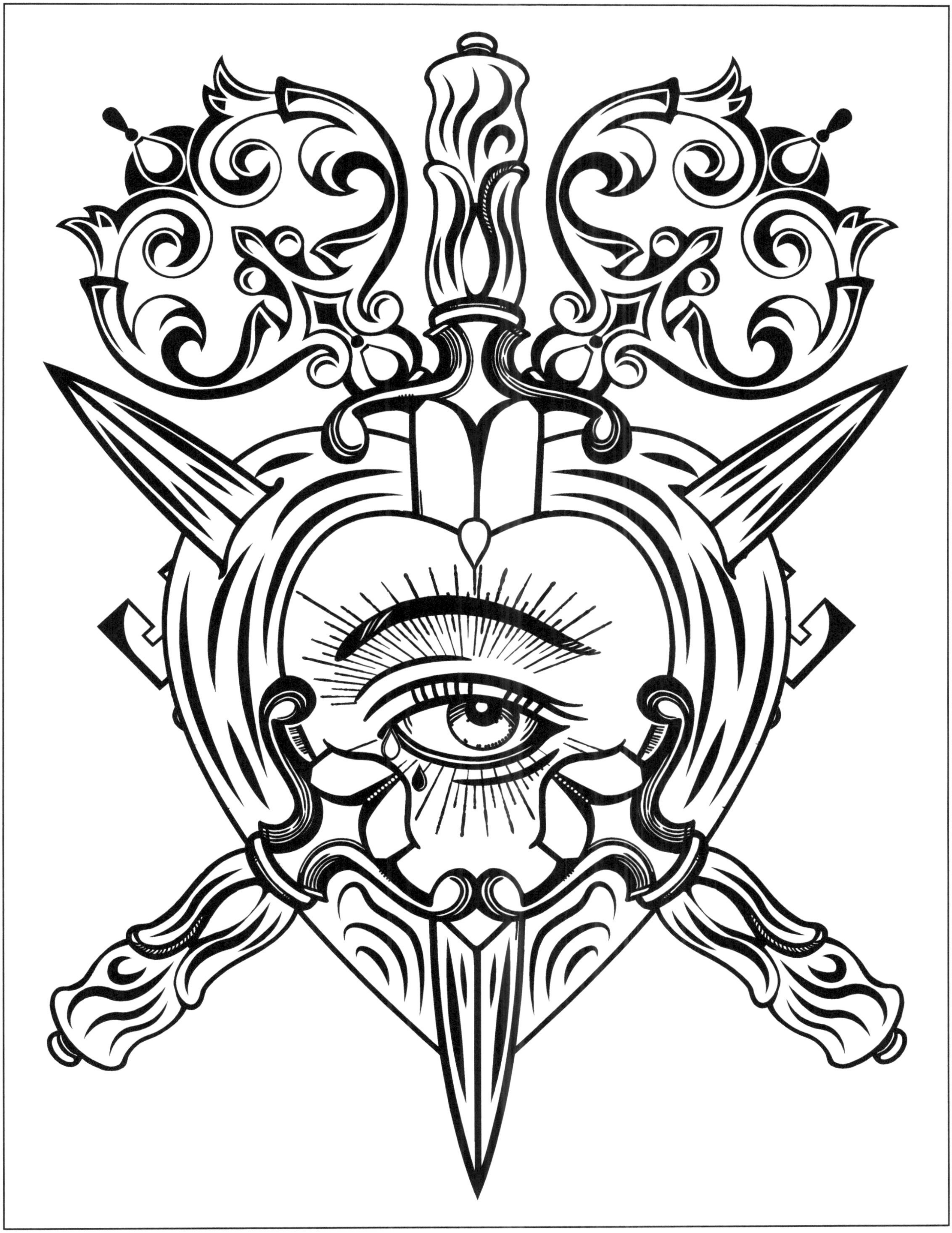

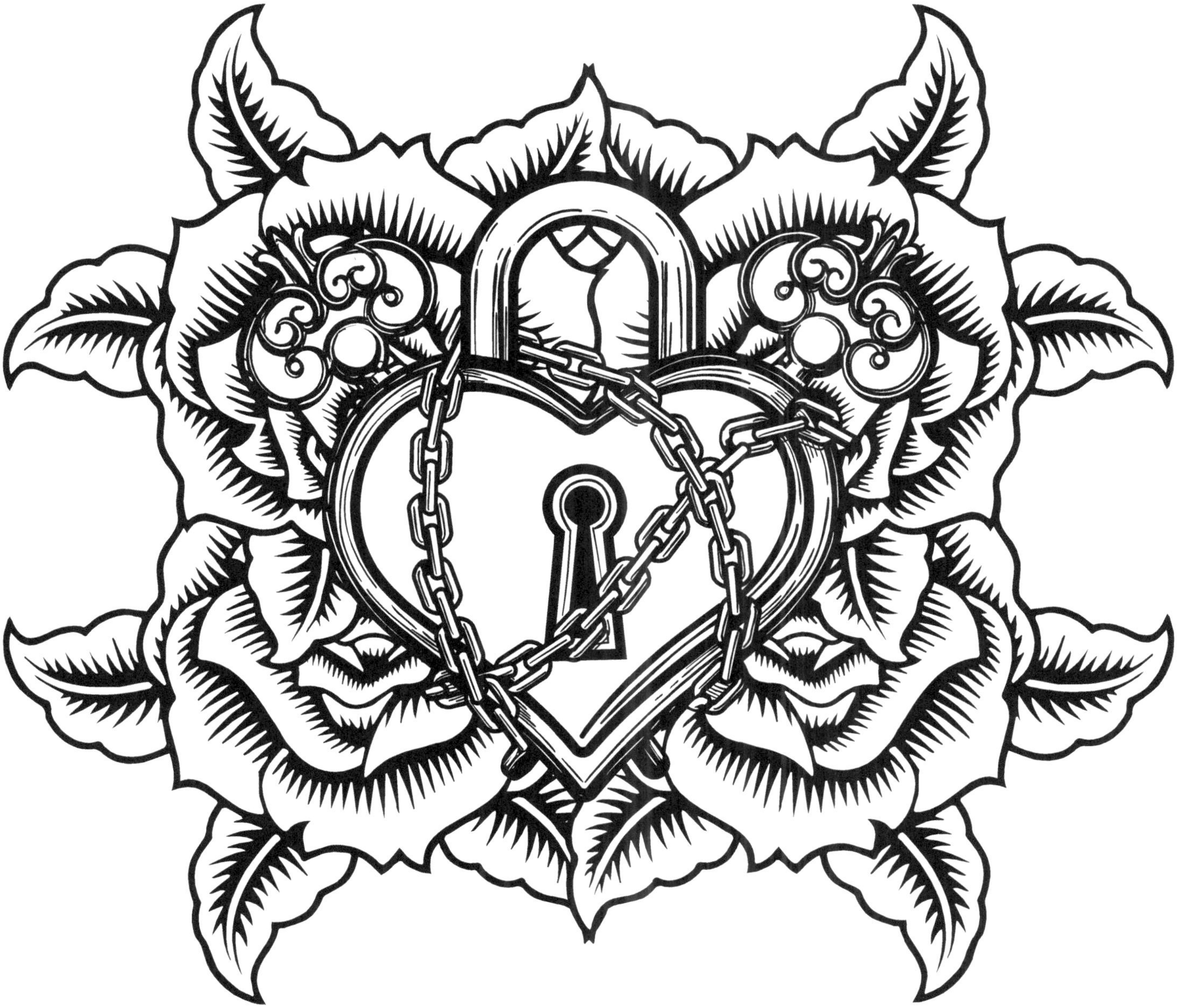

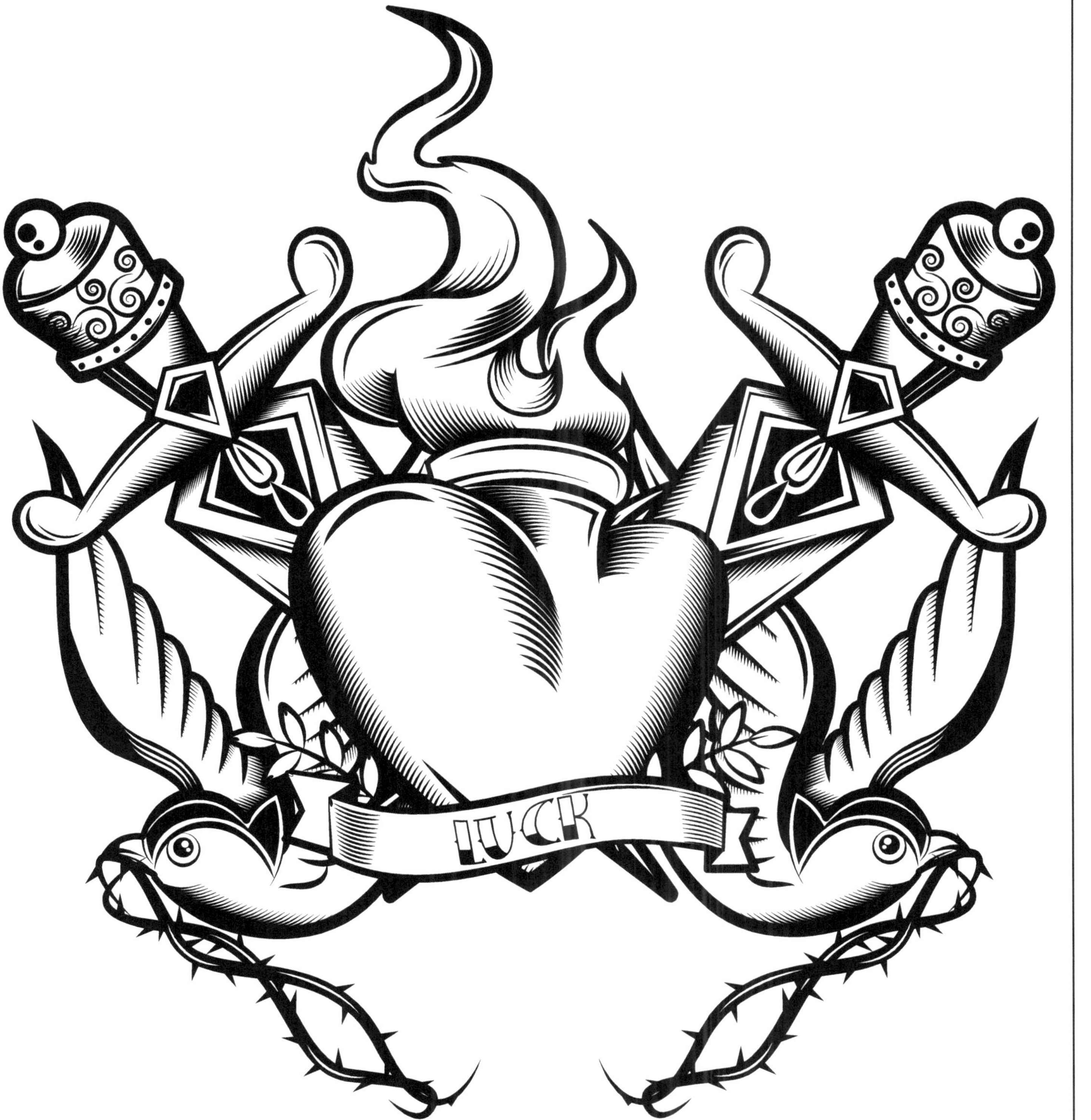
LUCK

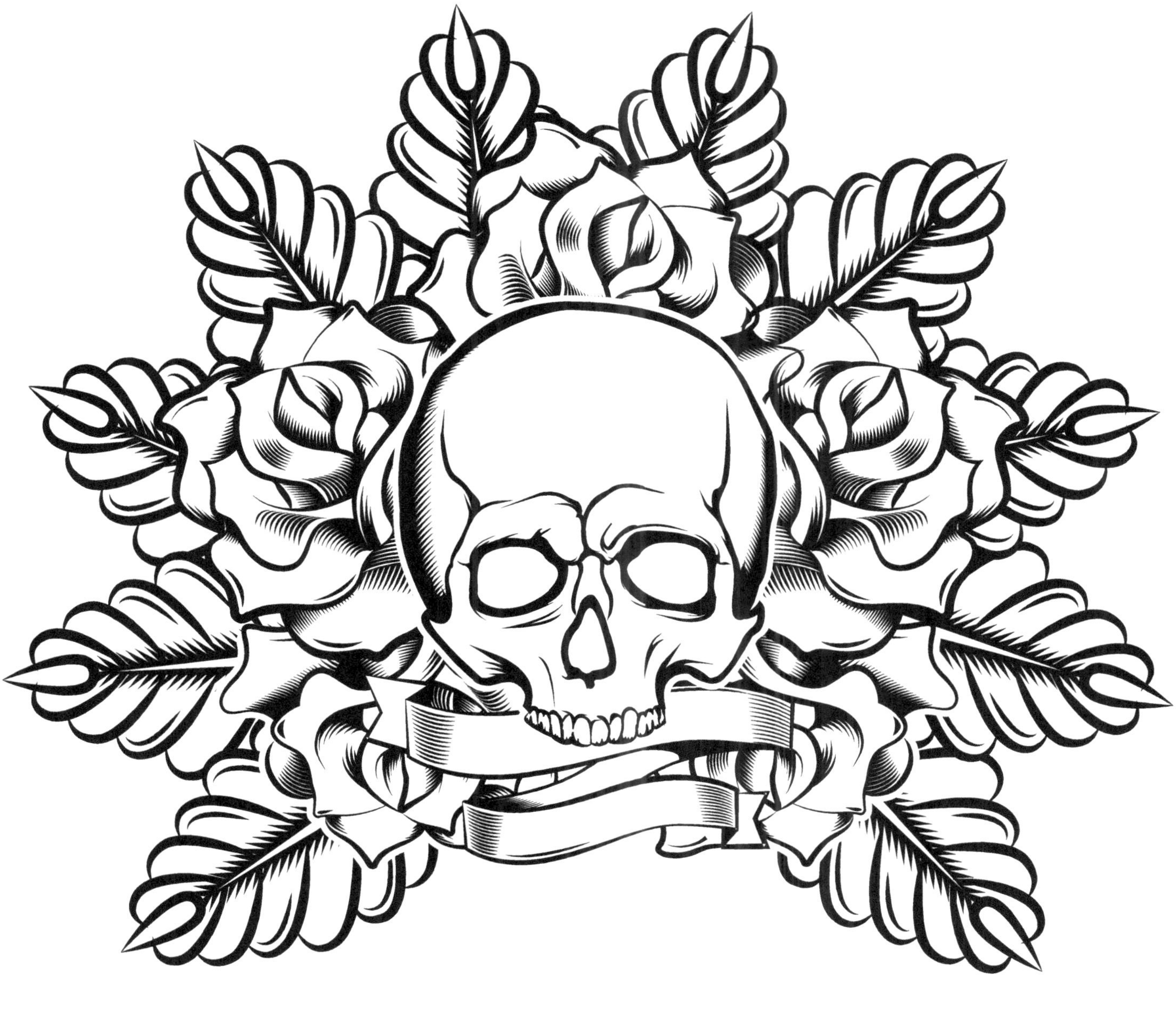

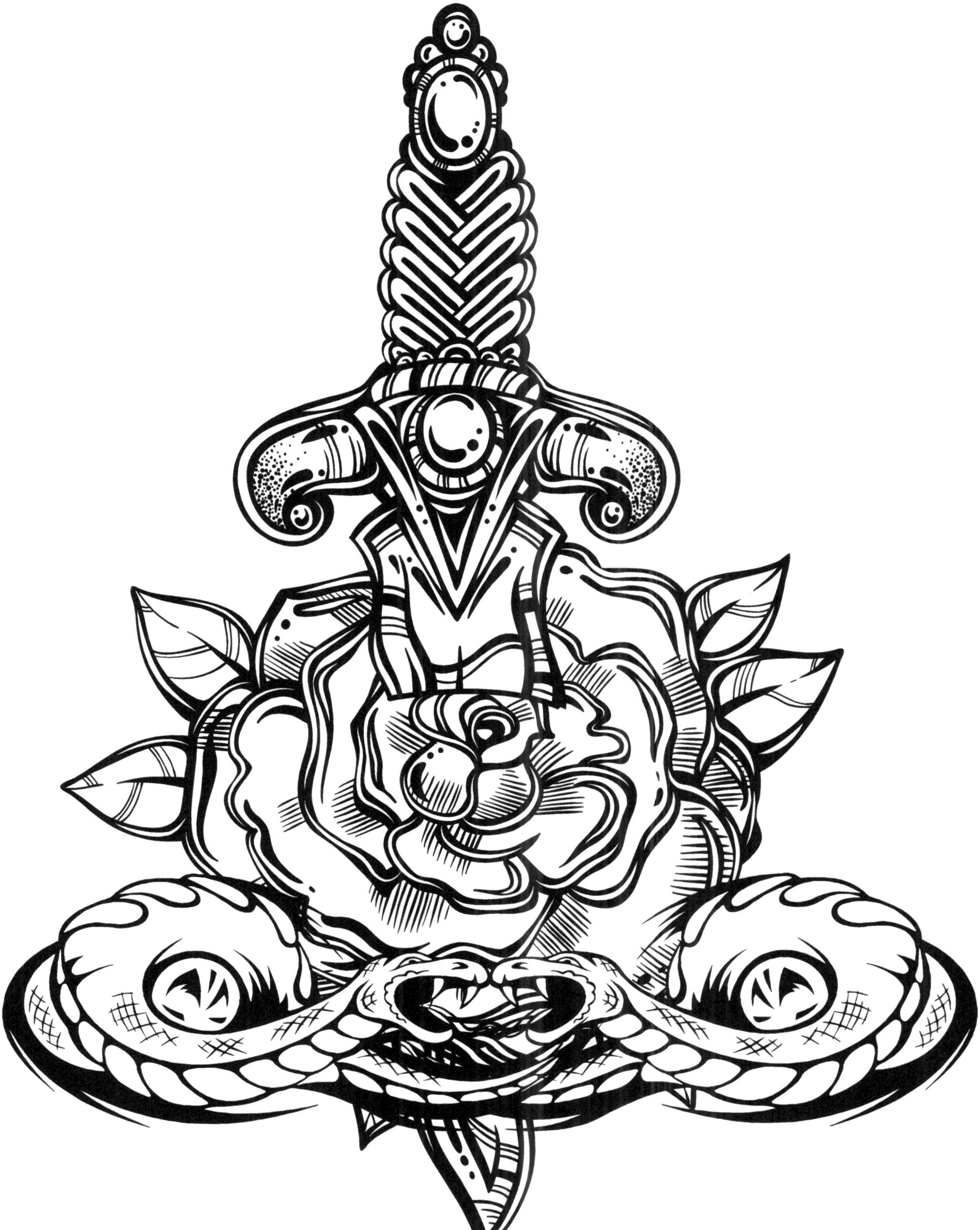

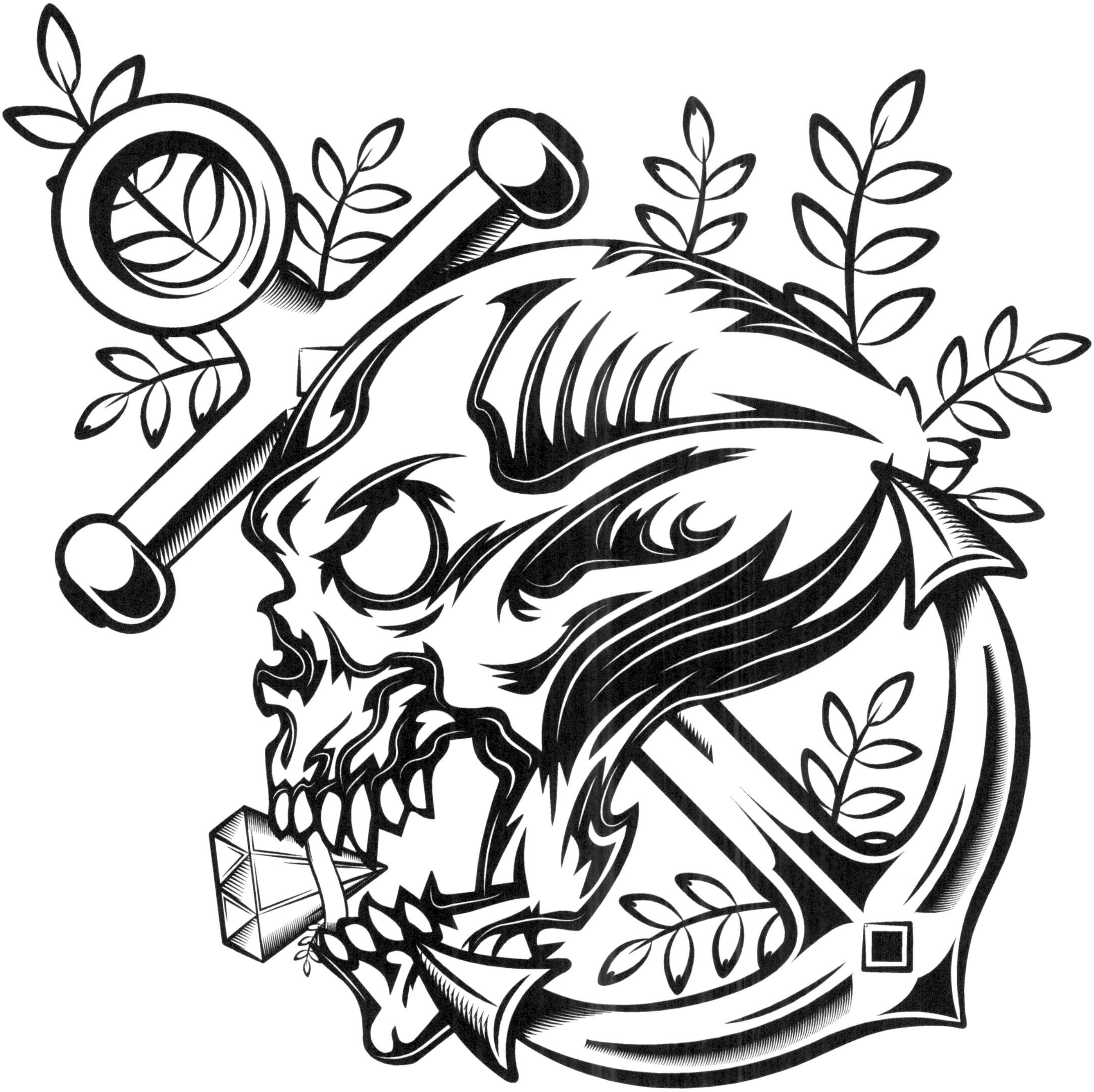

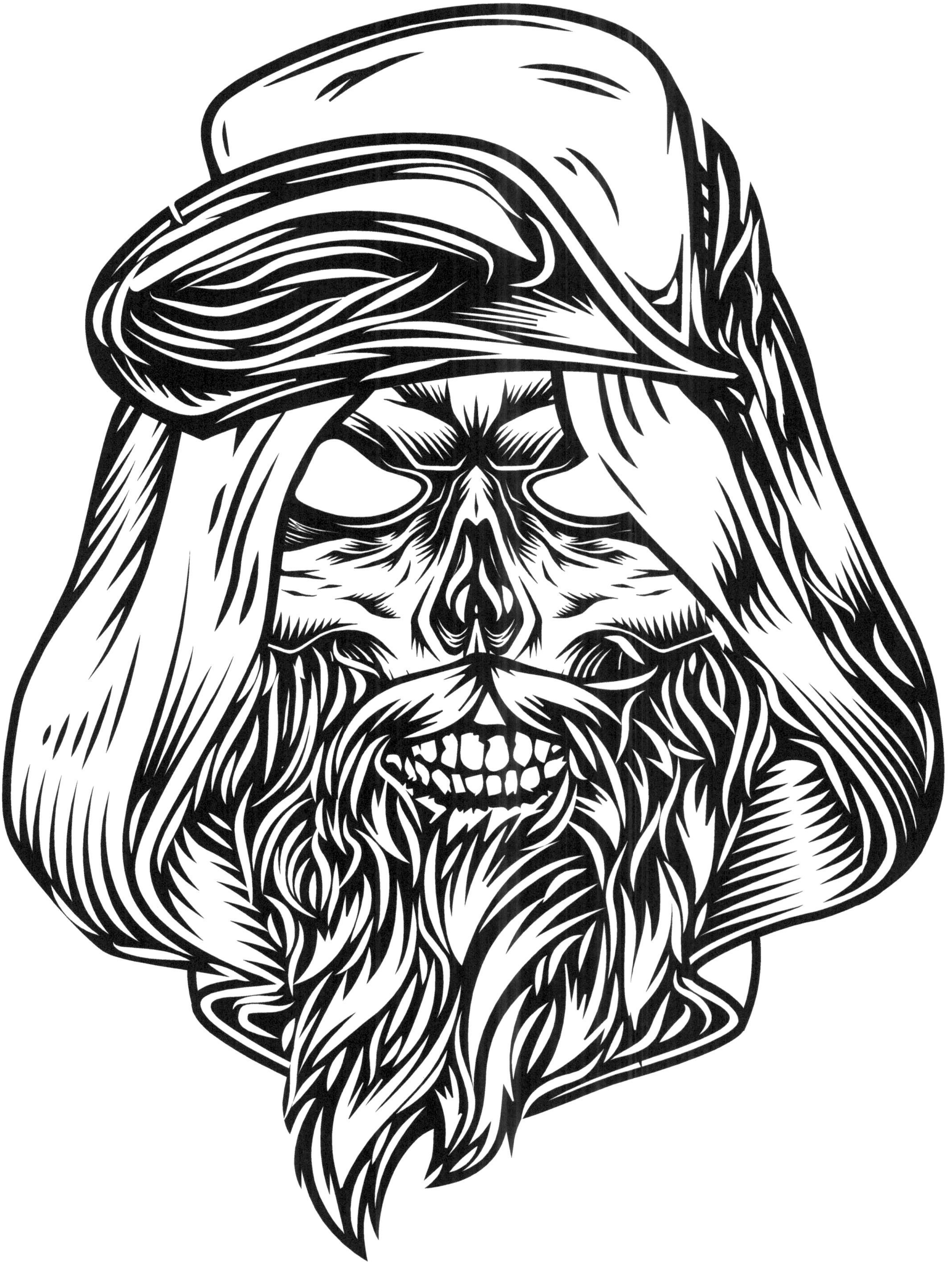

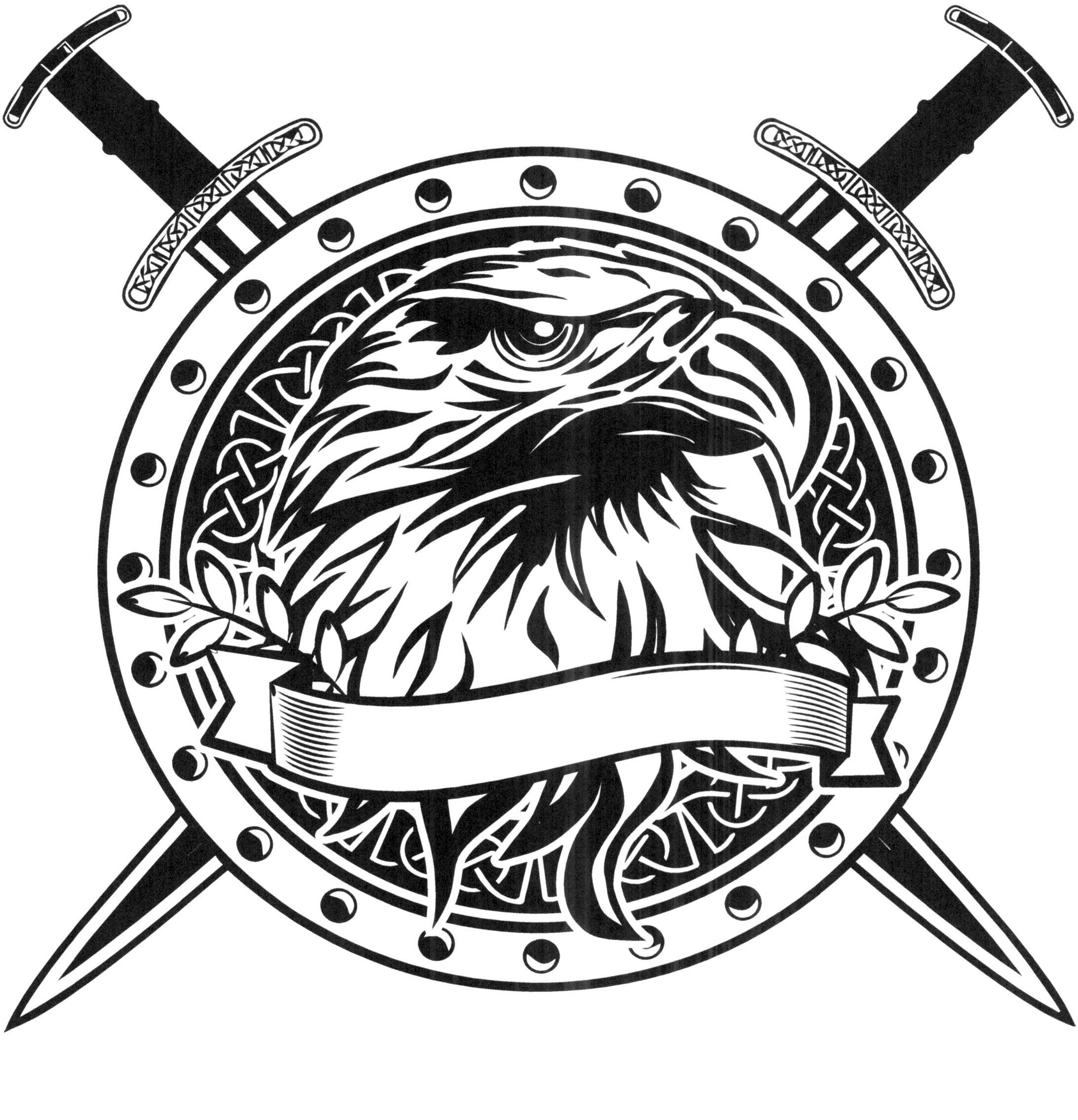

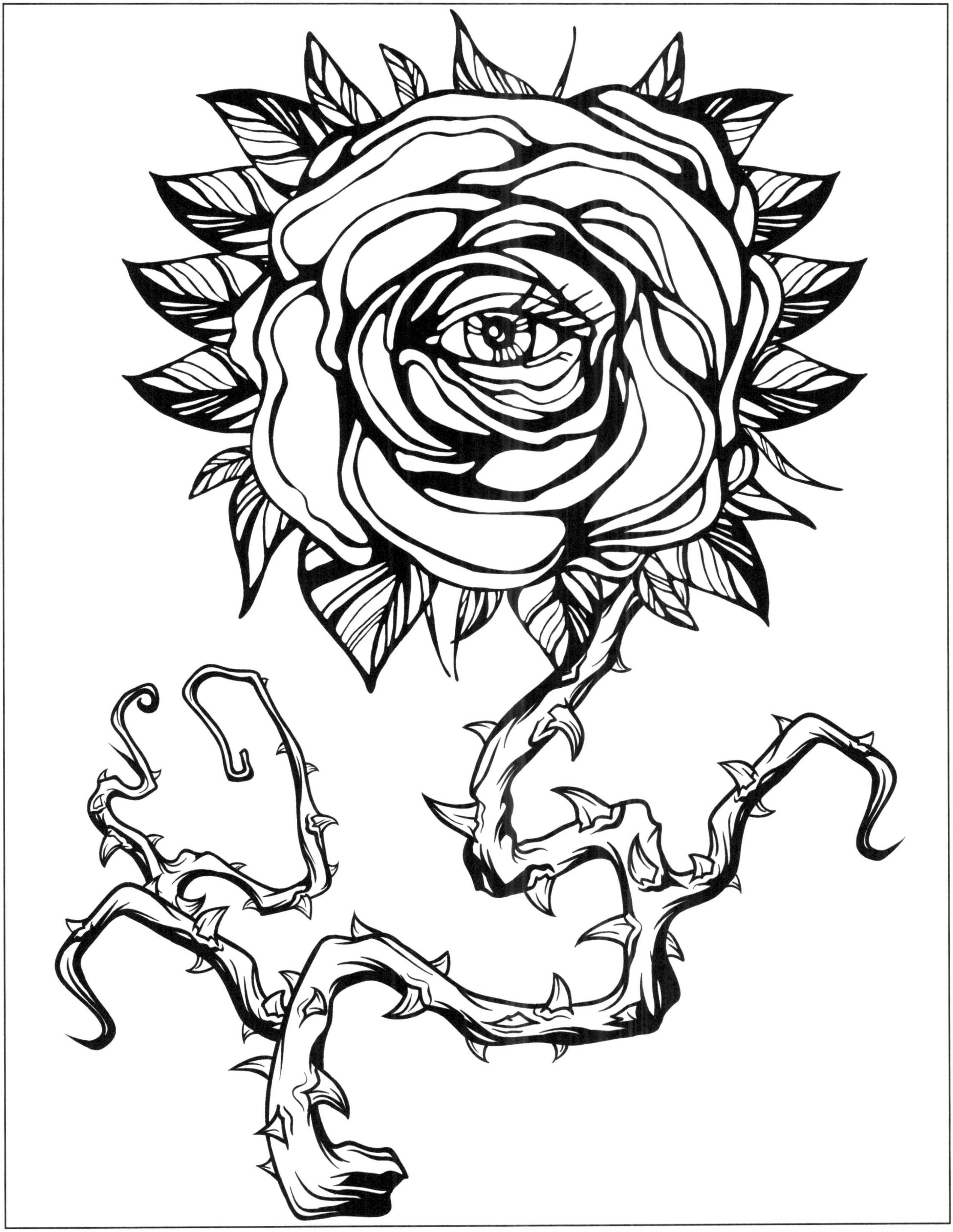

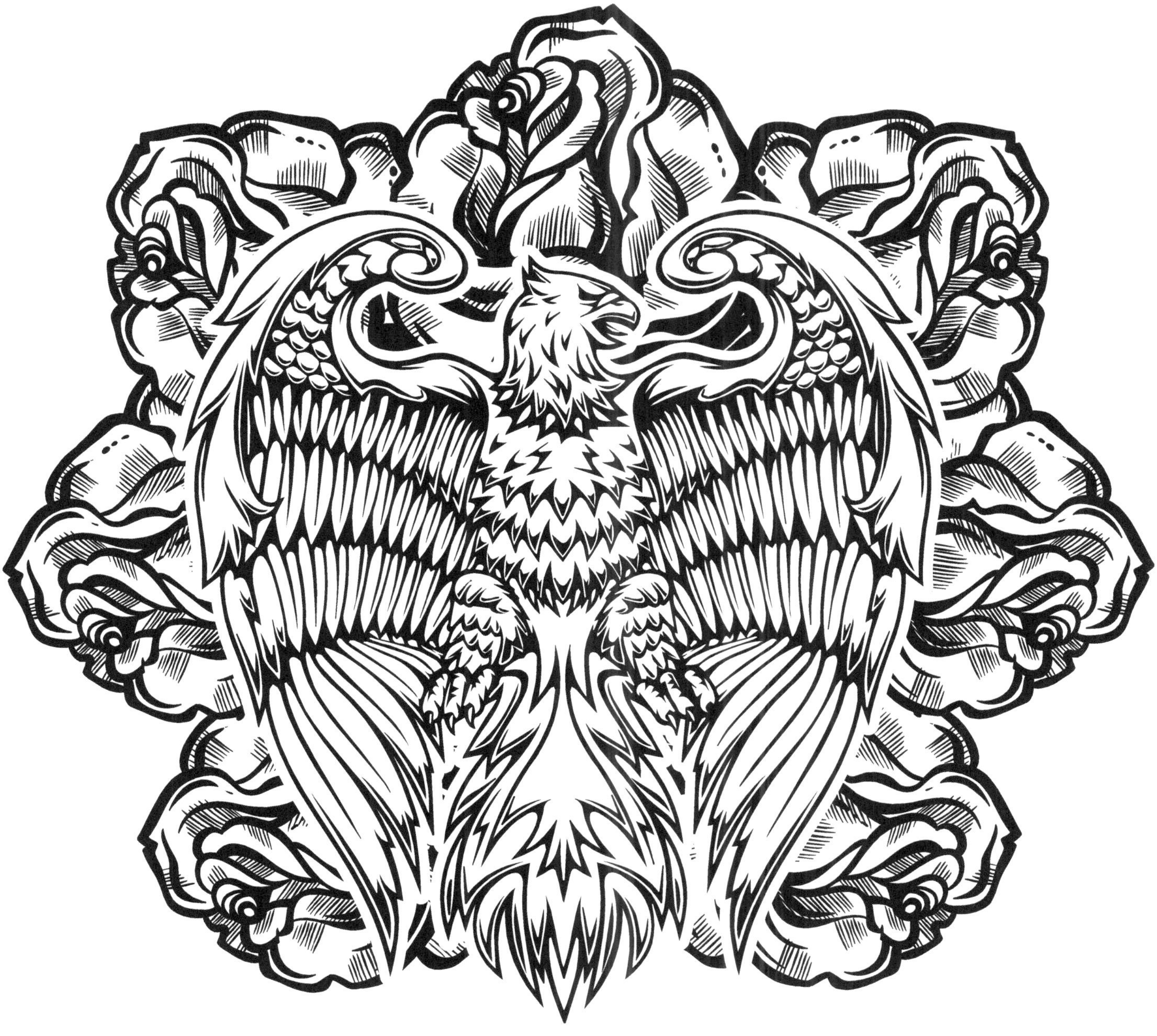

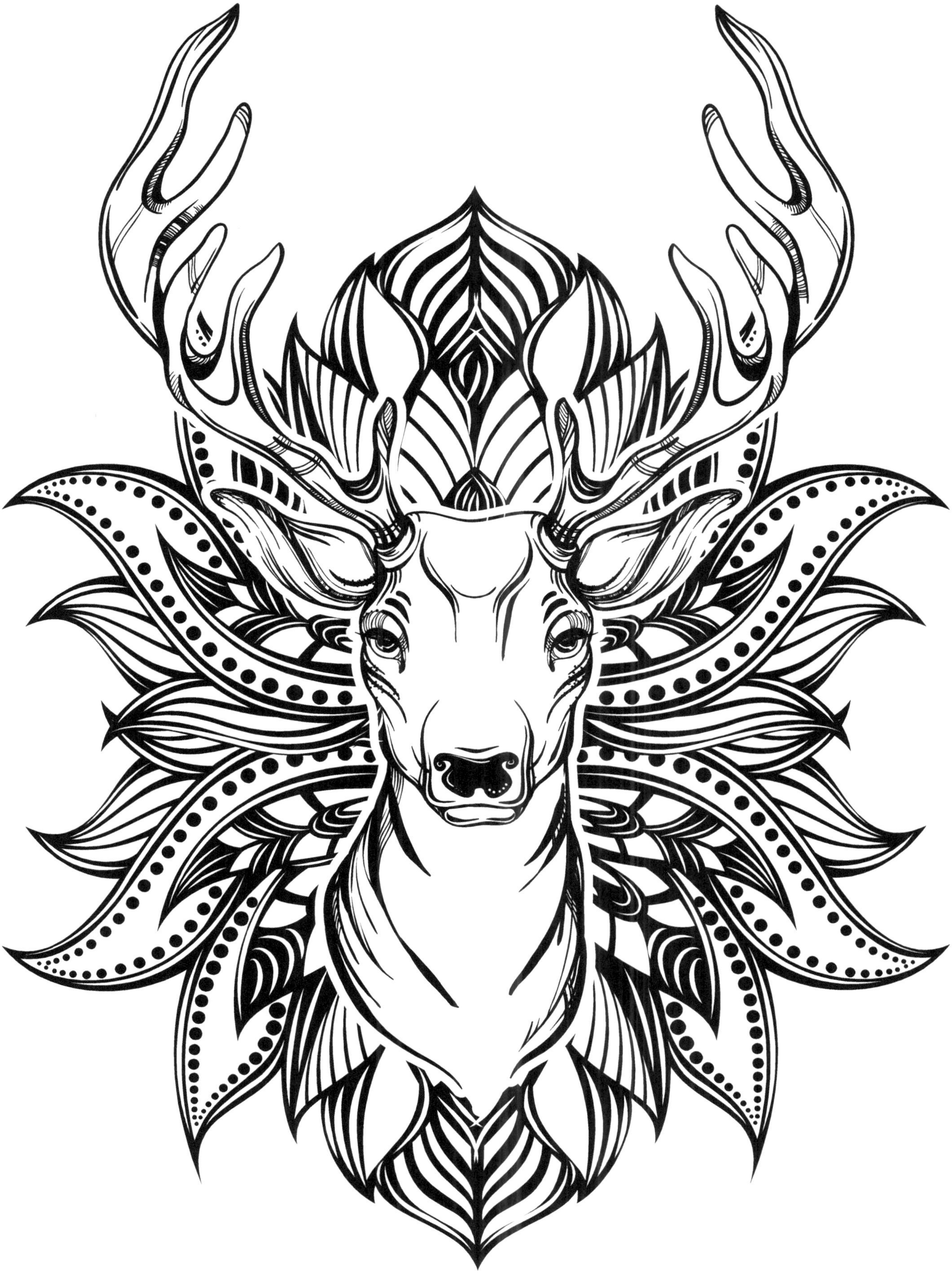

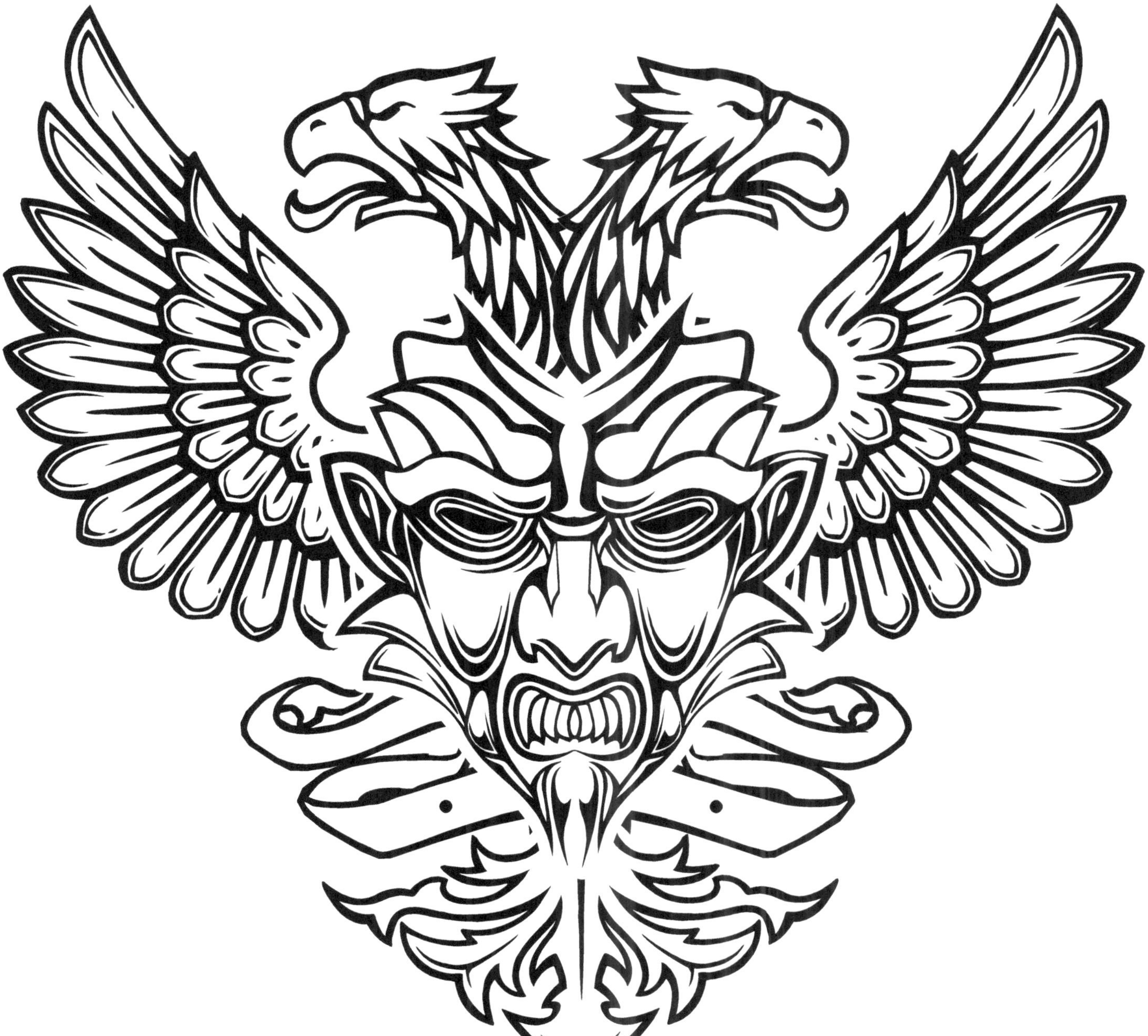

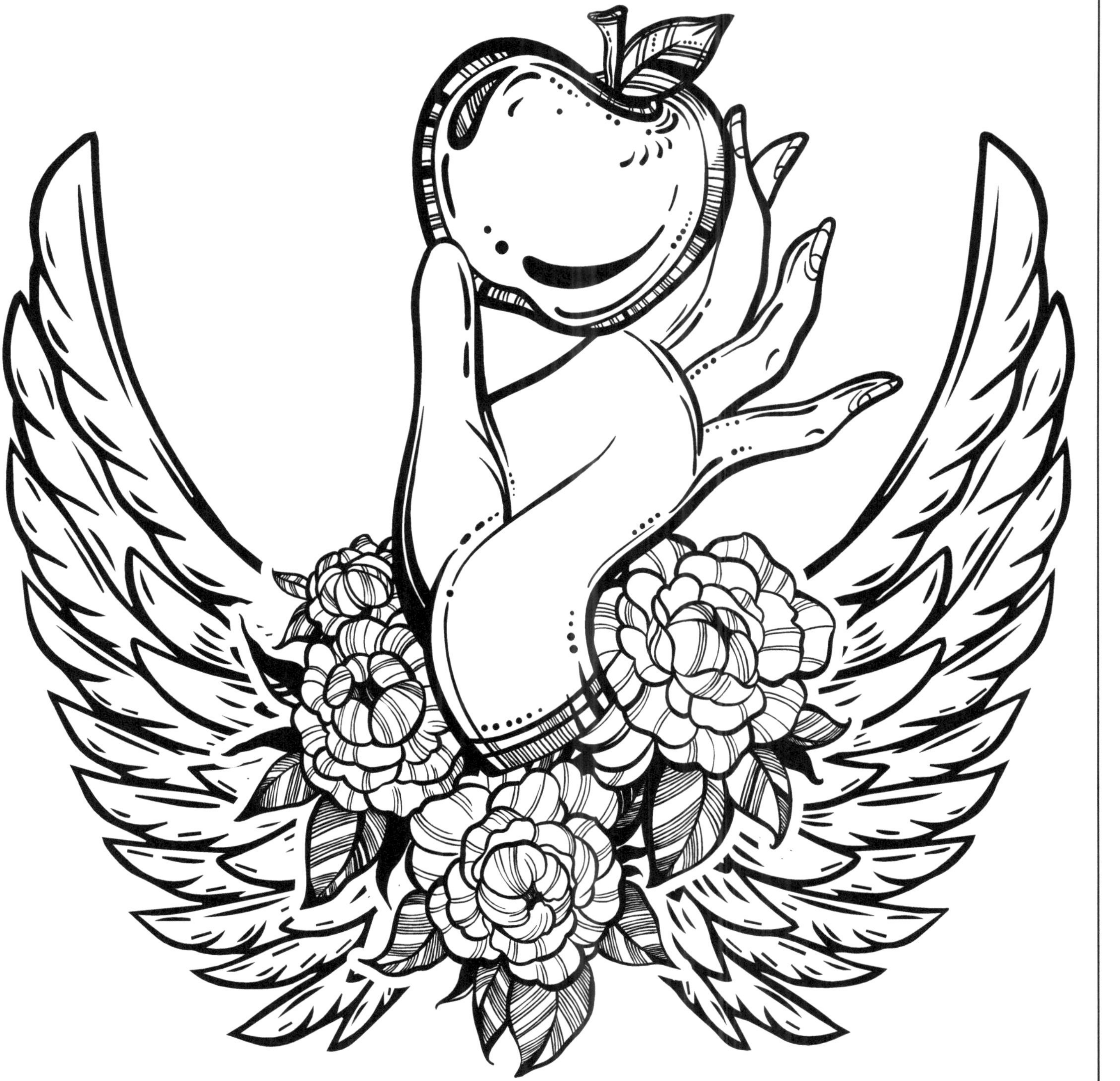

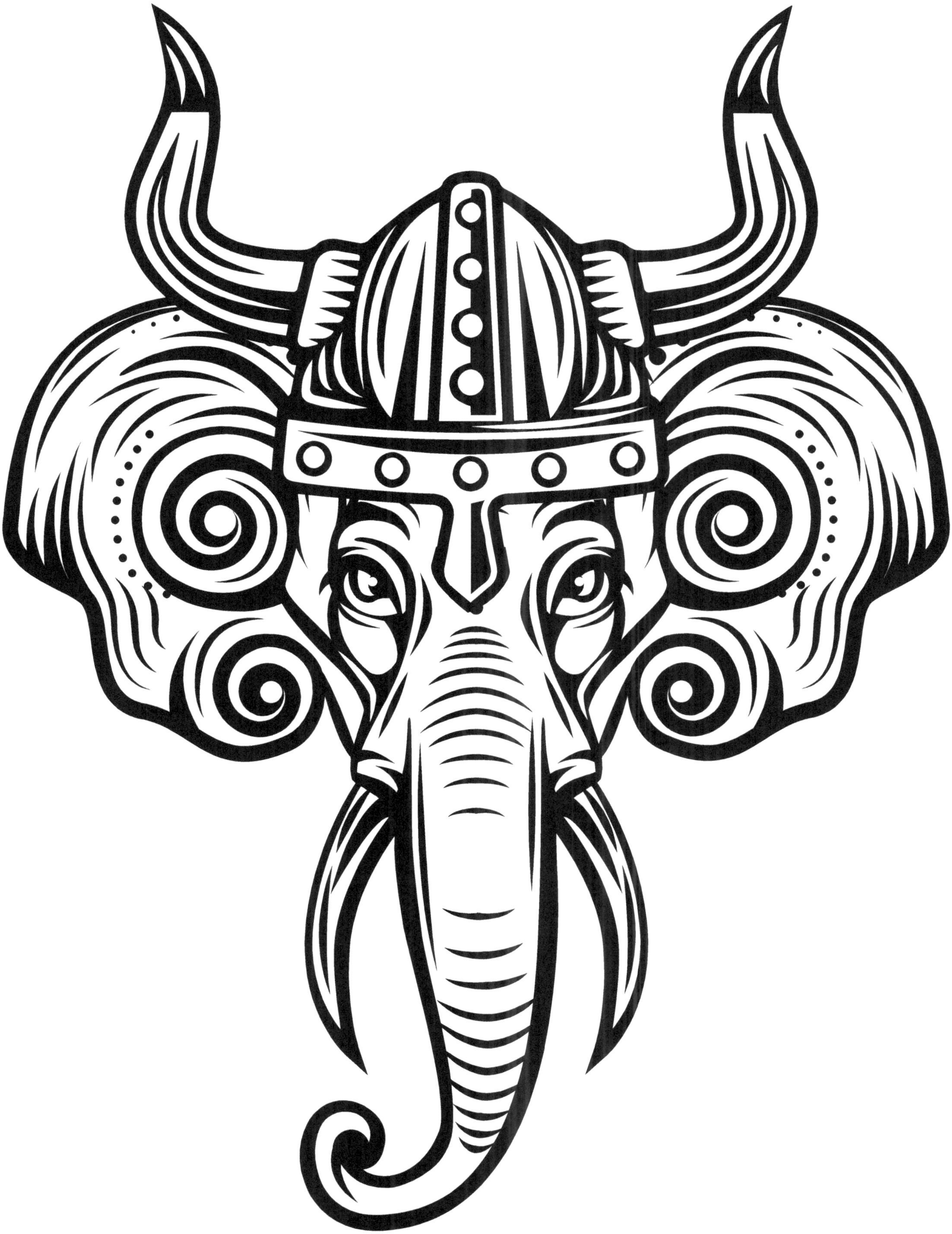

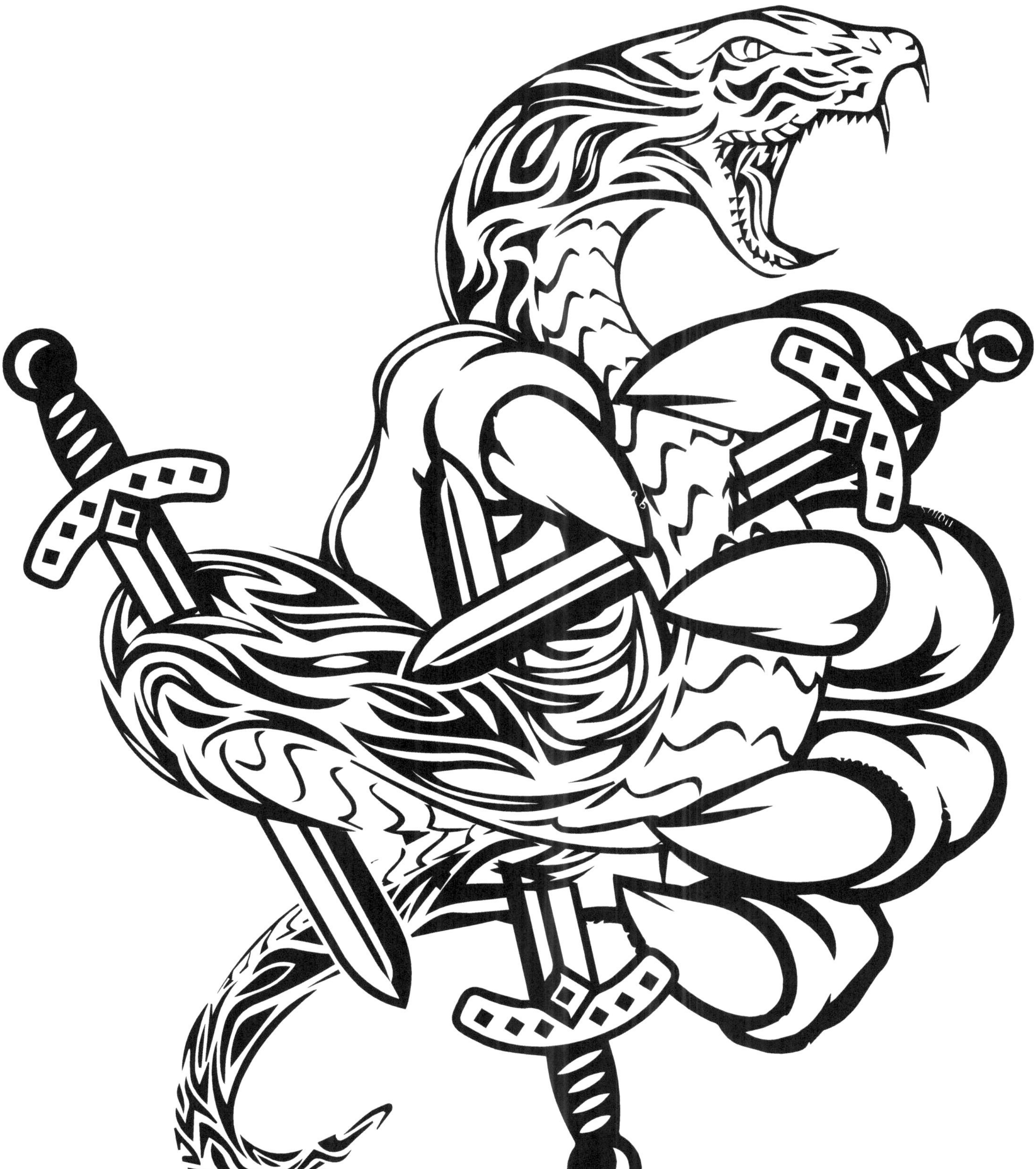

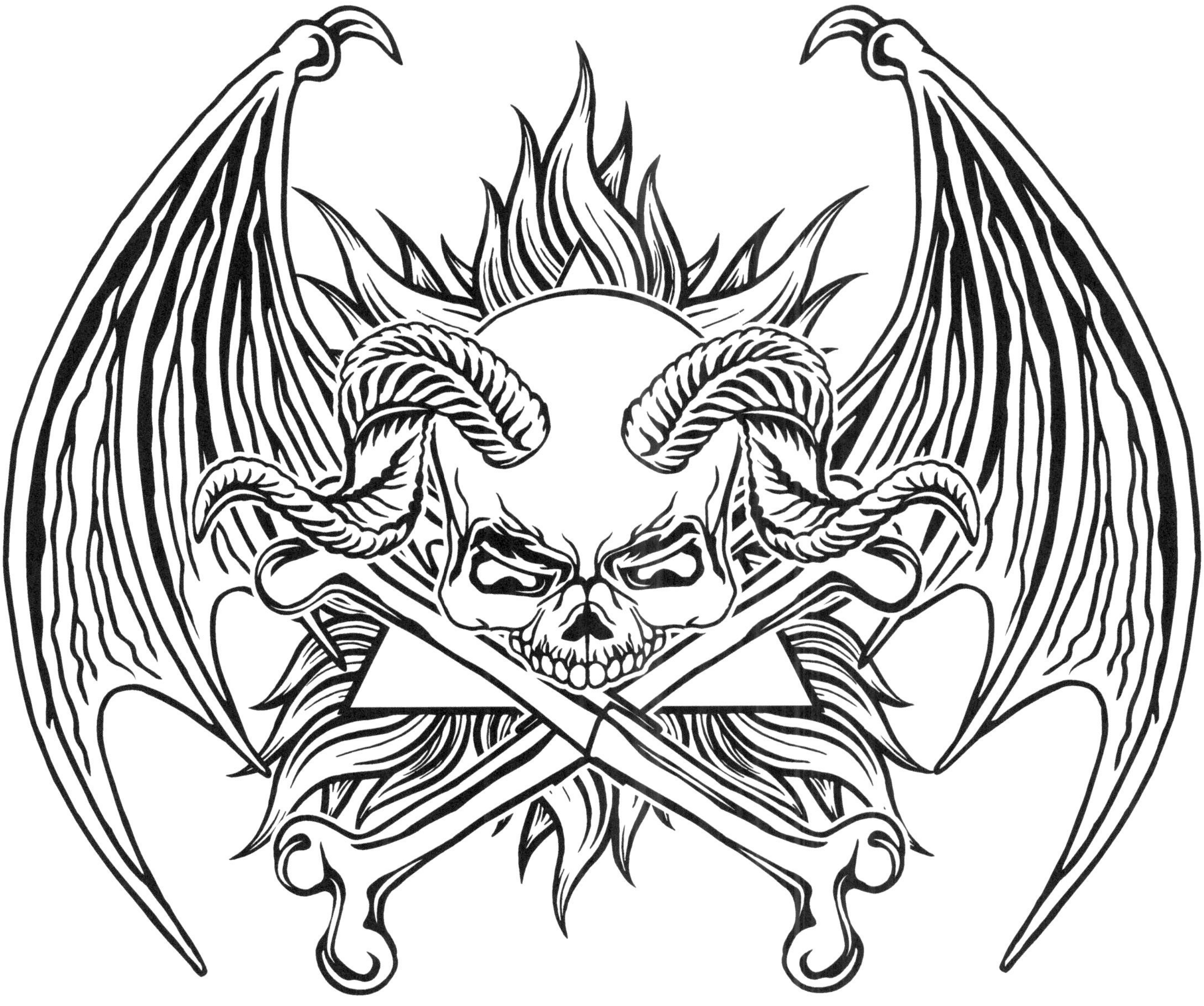

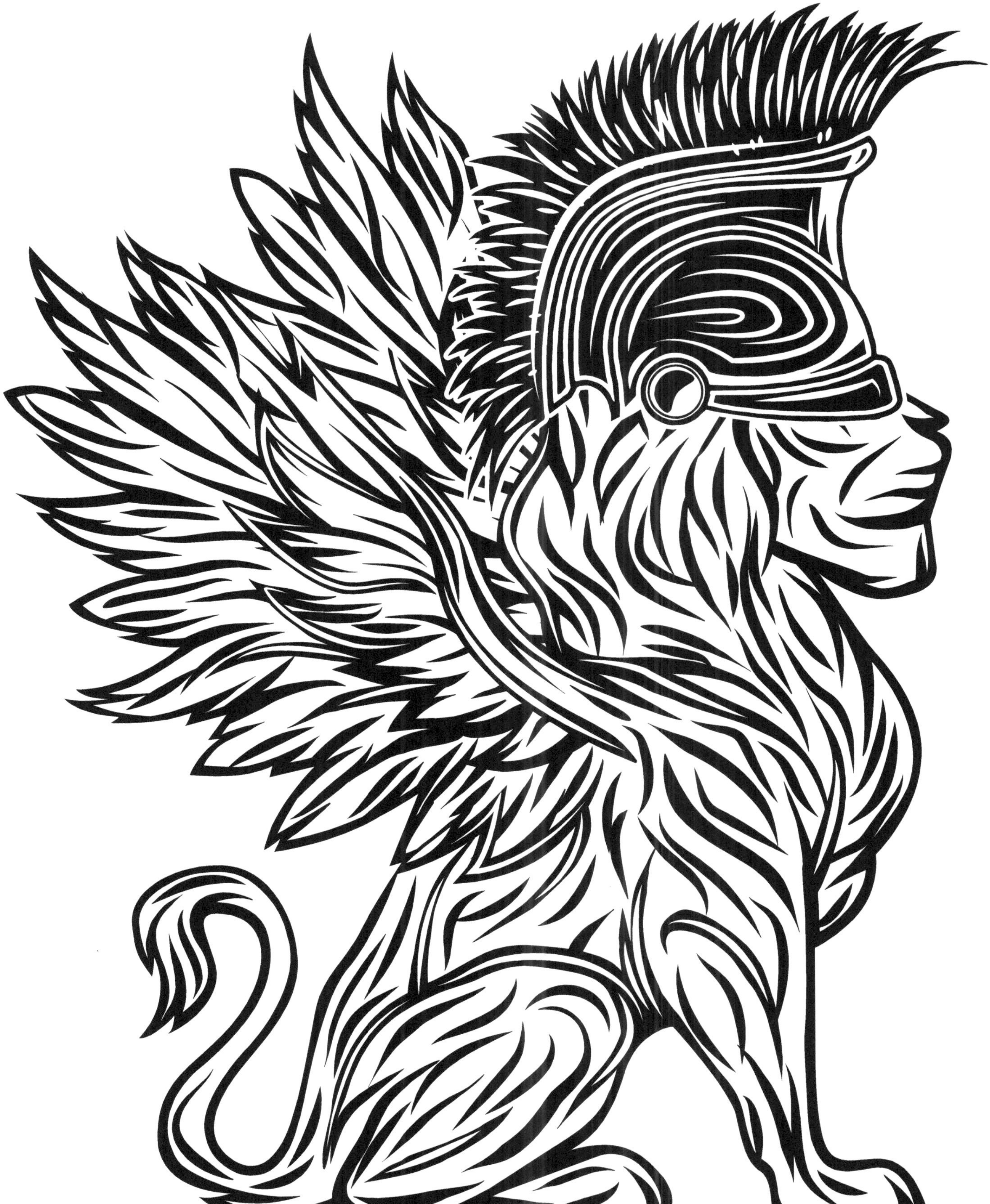

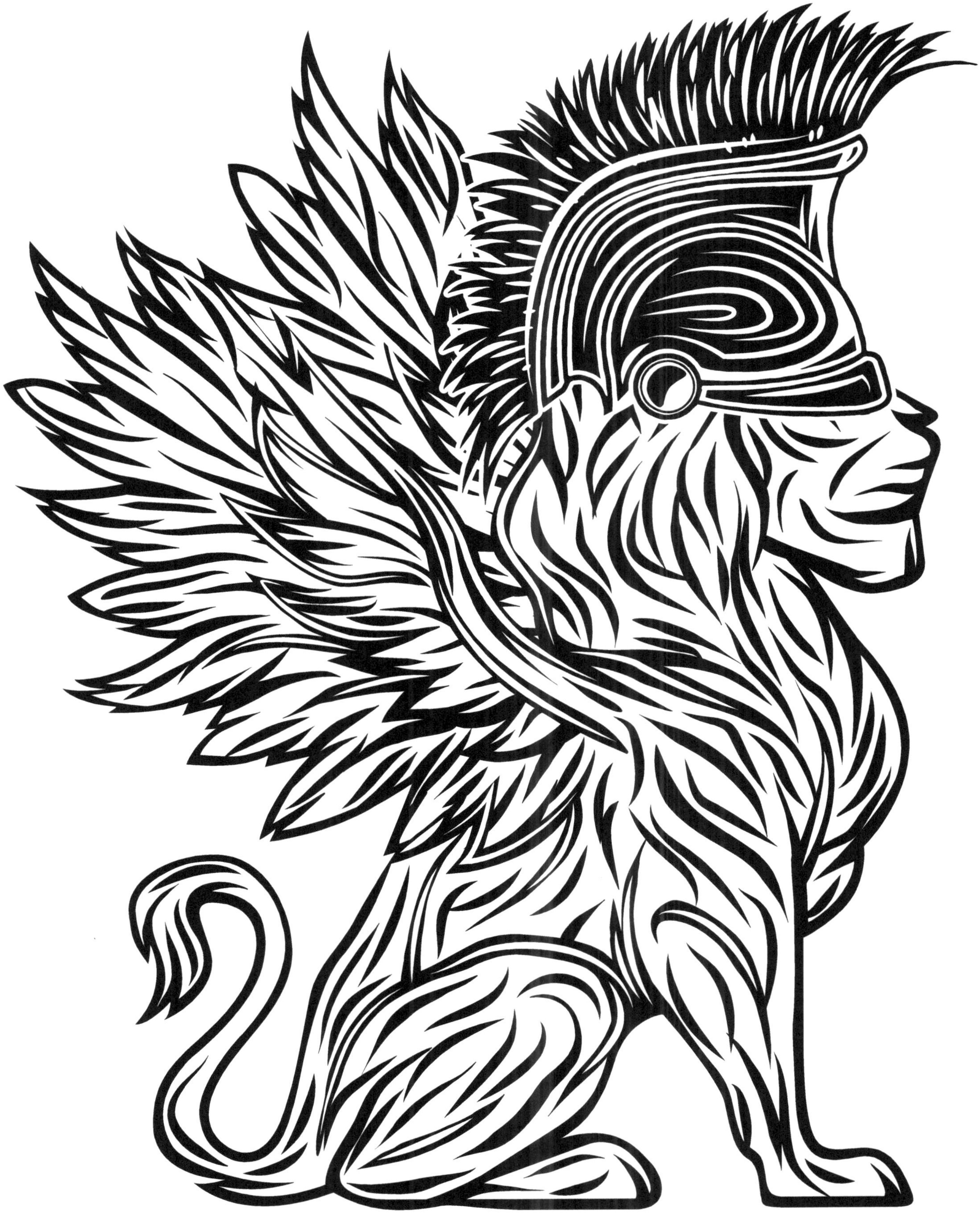

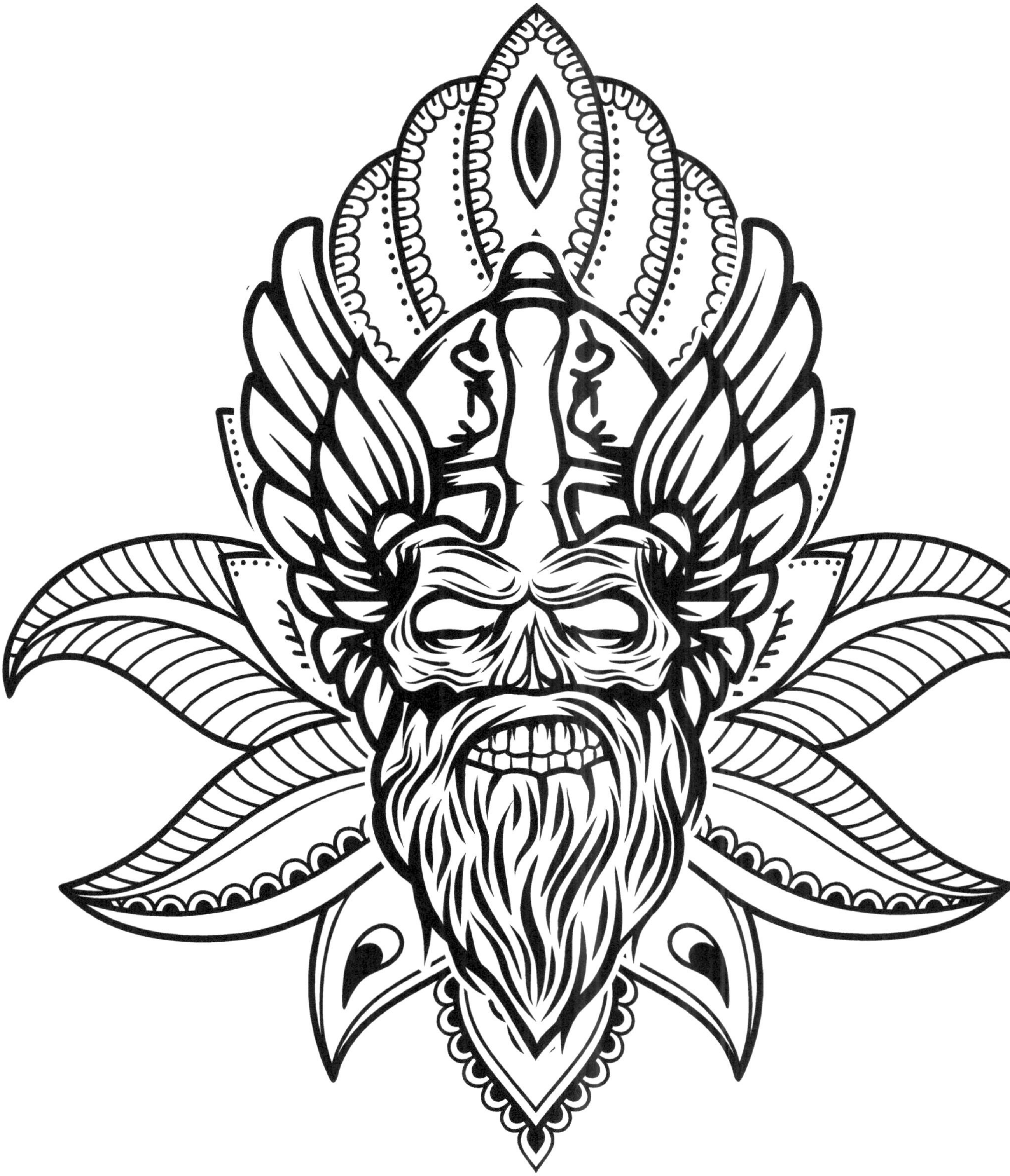

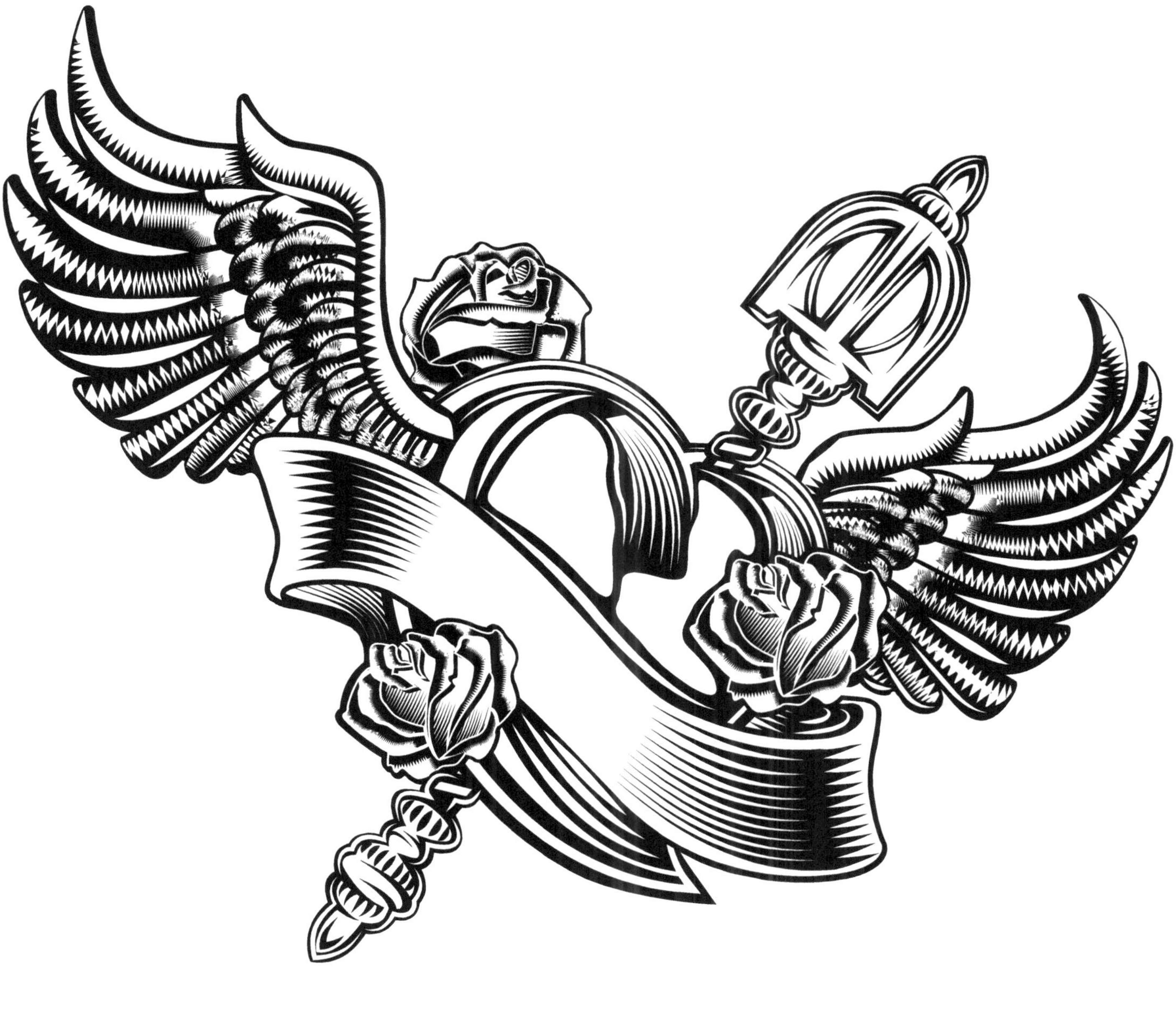

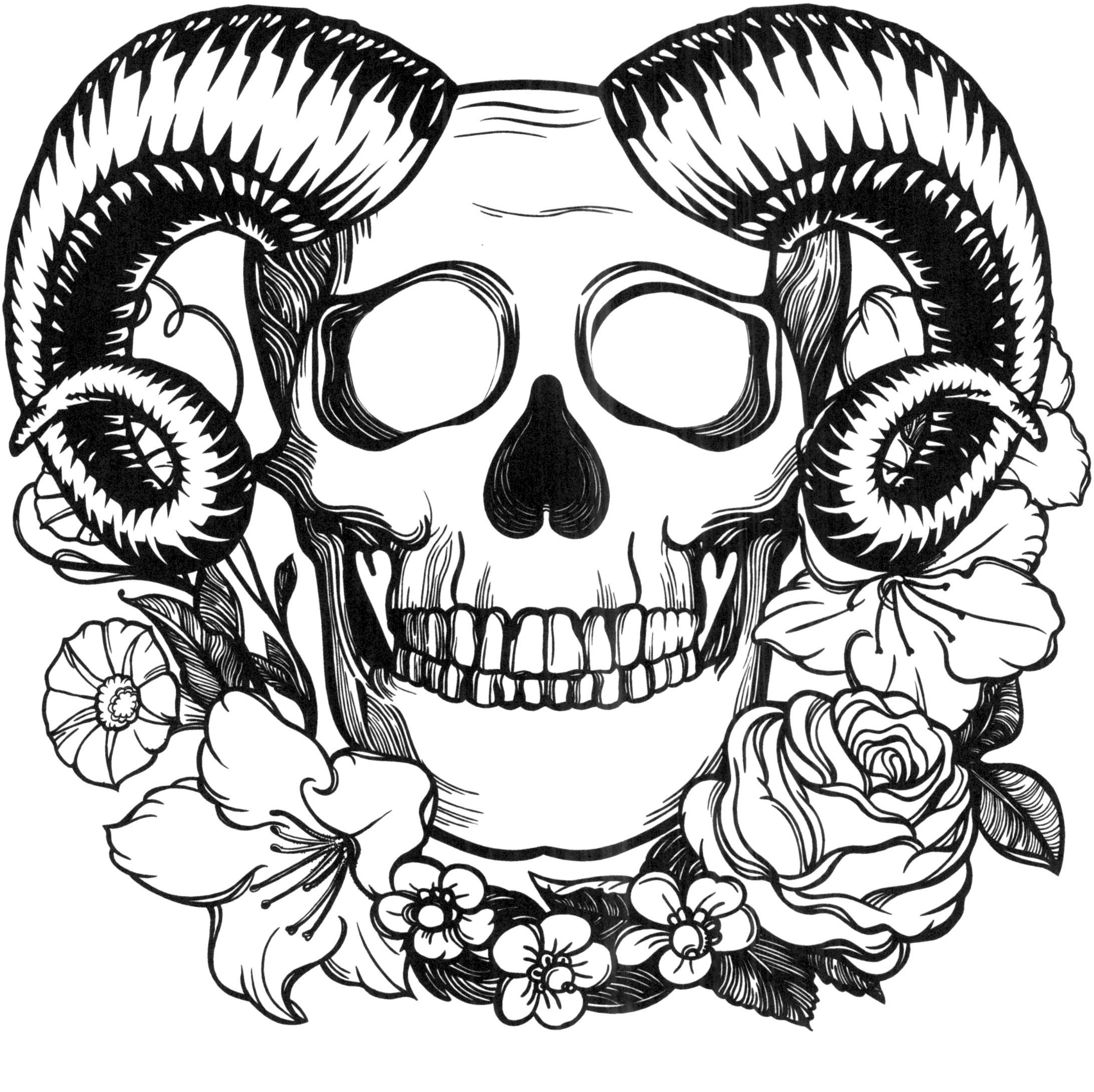

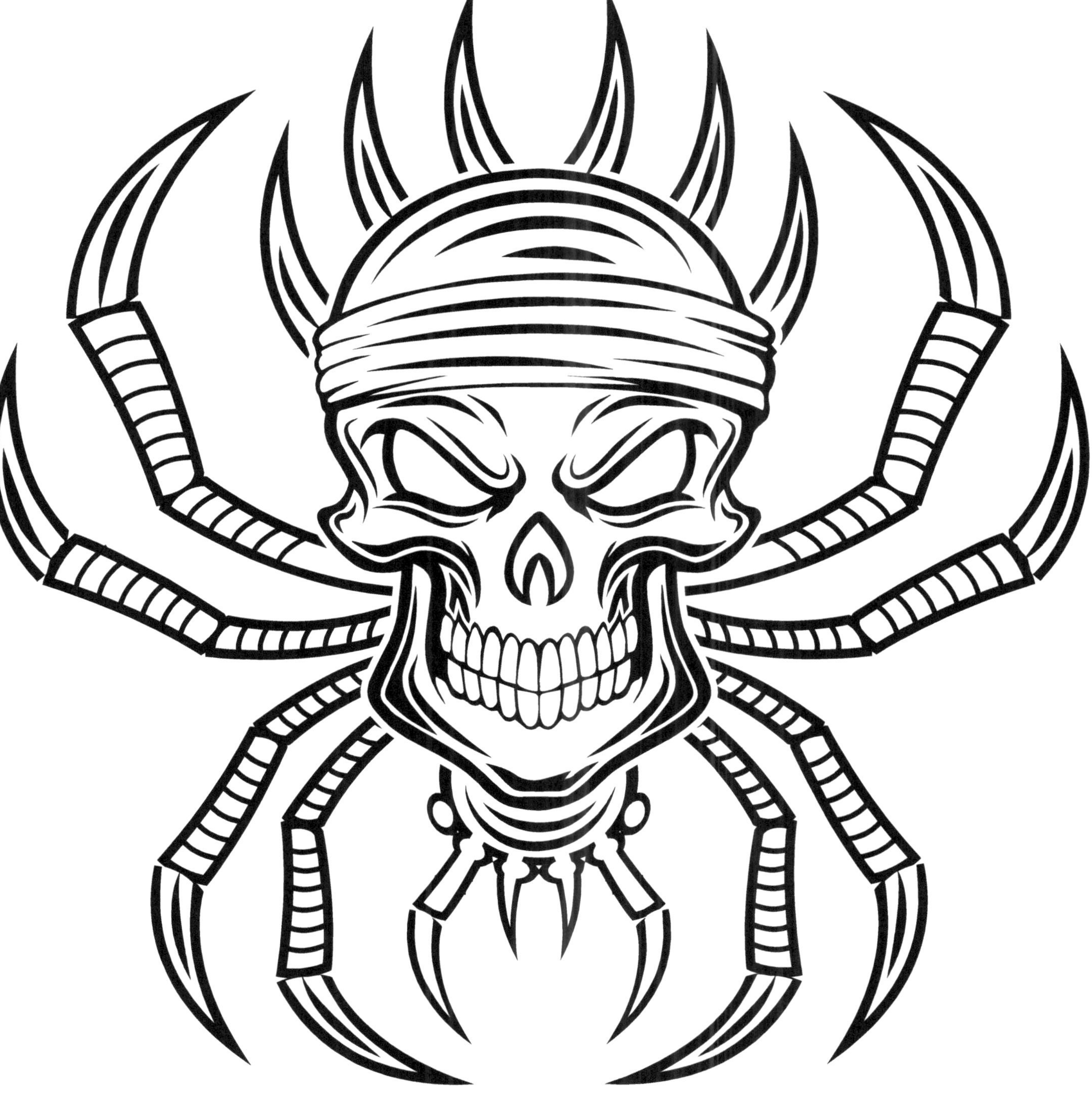

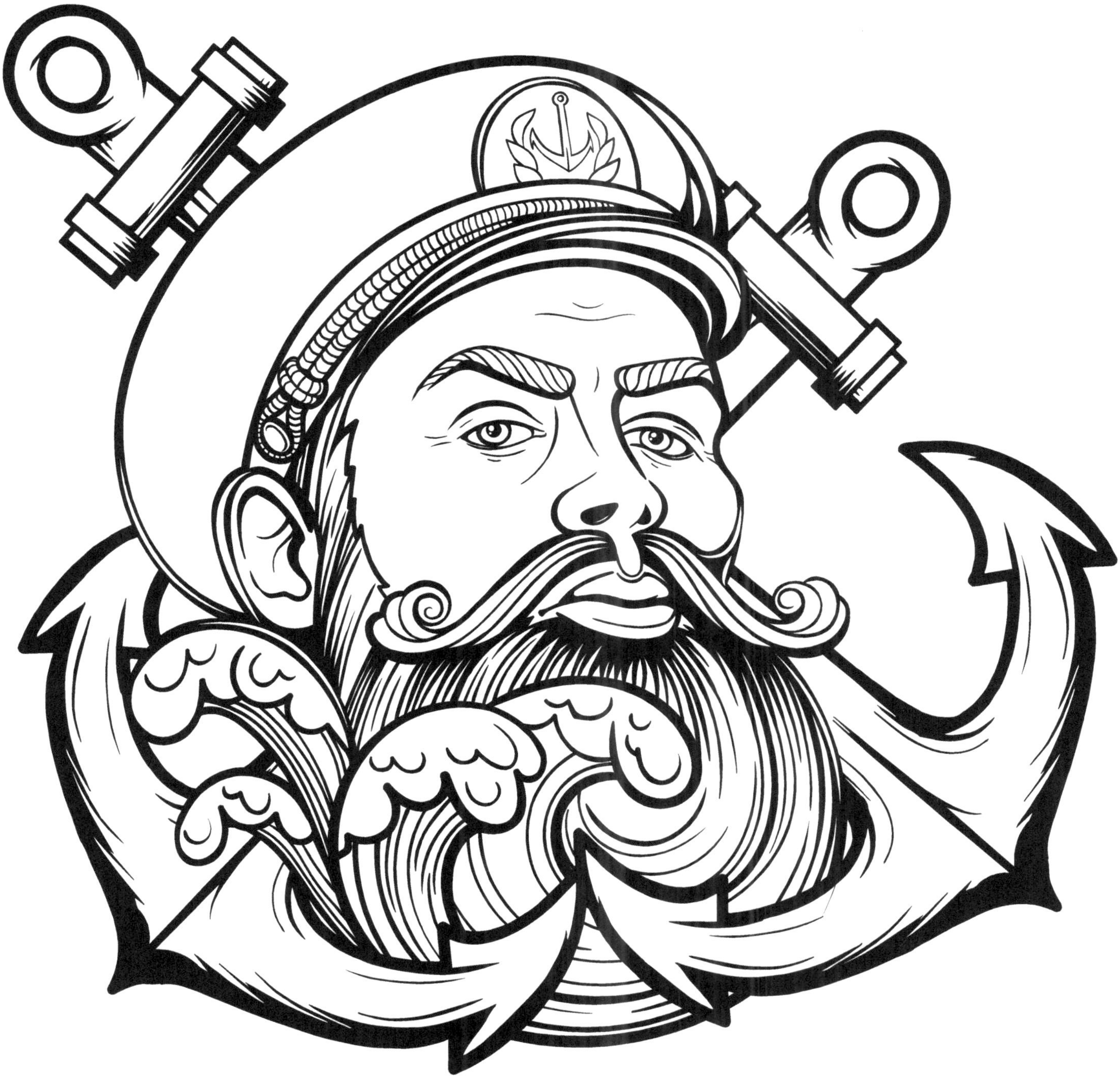

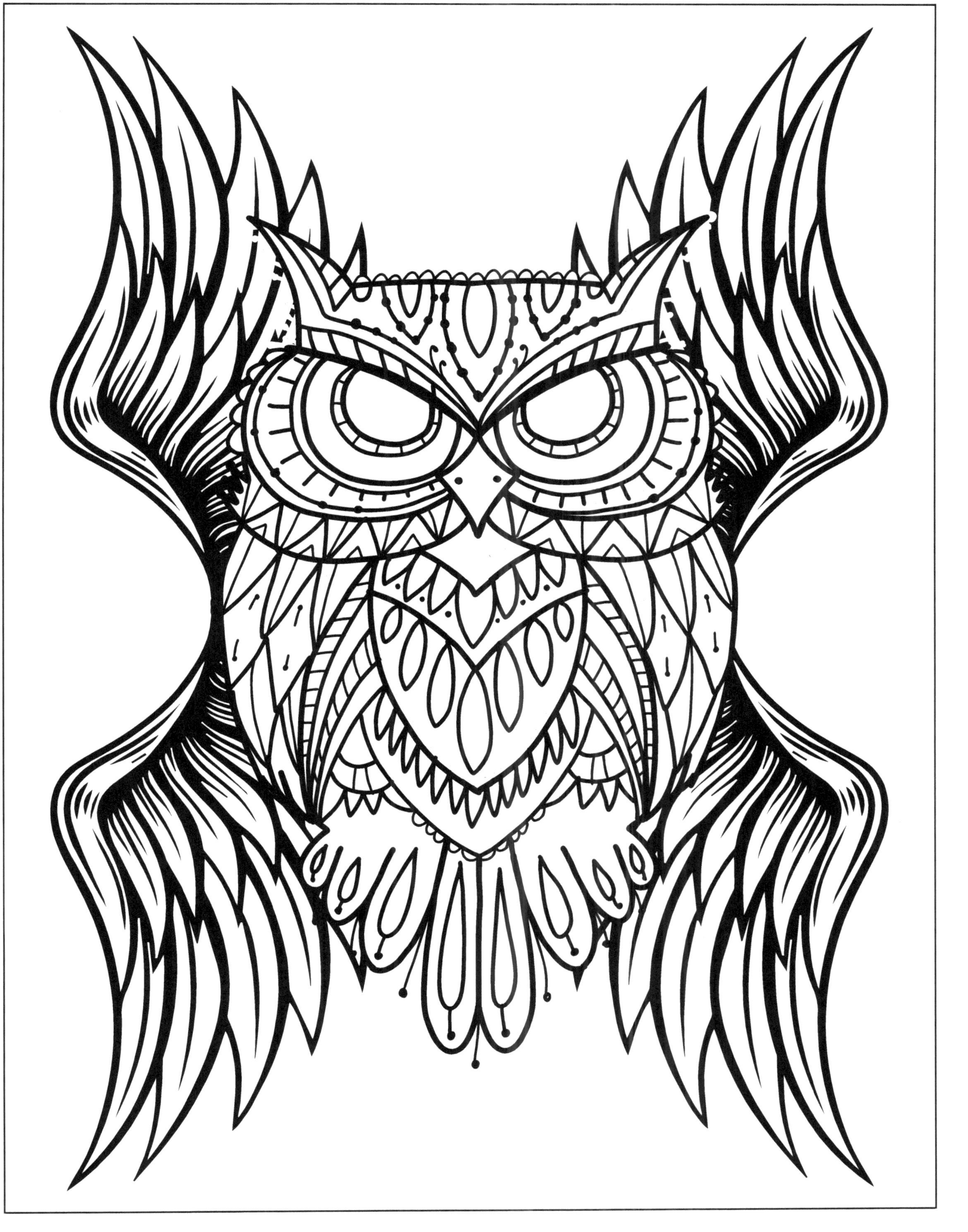

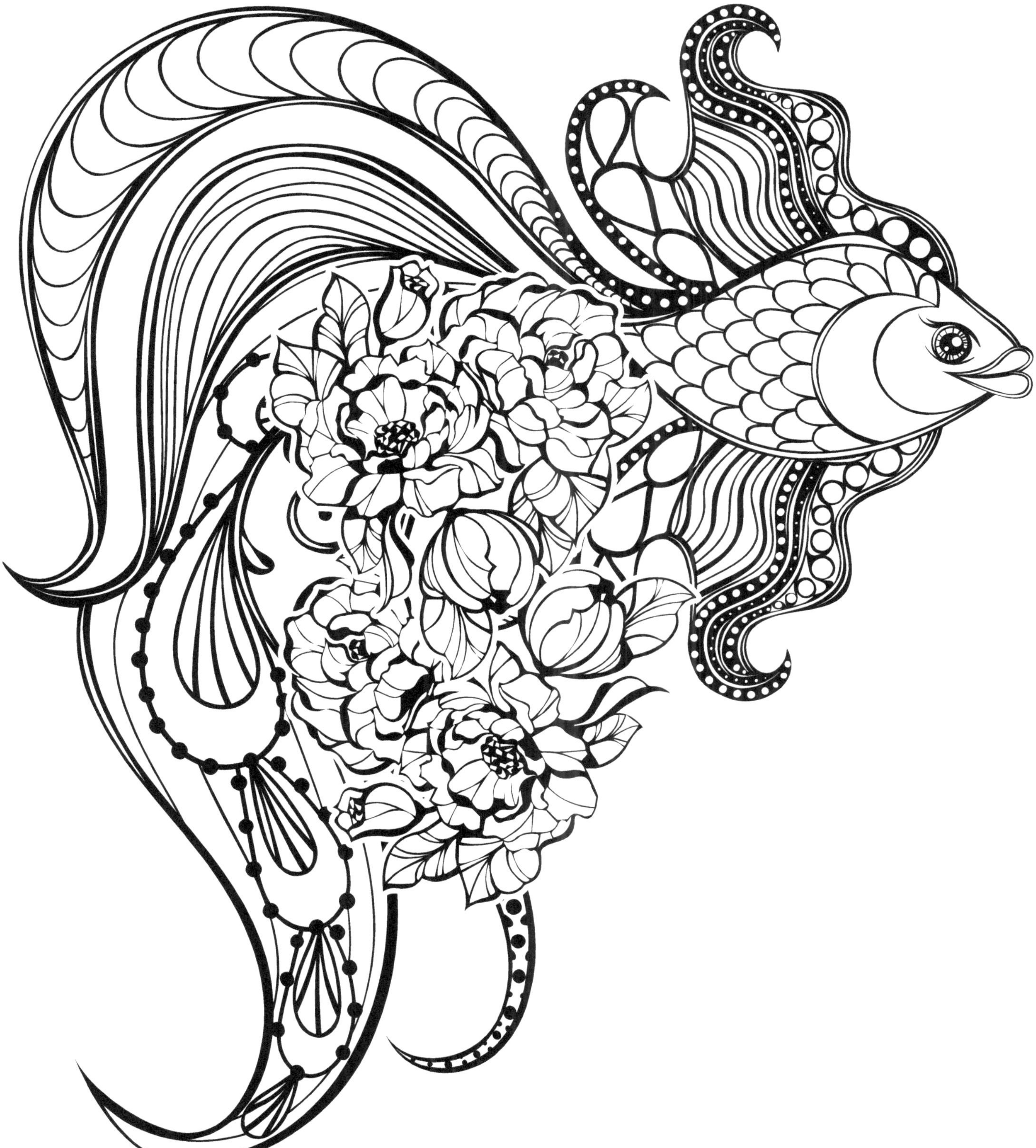

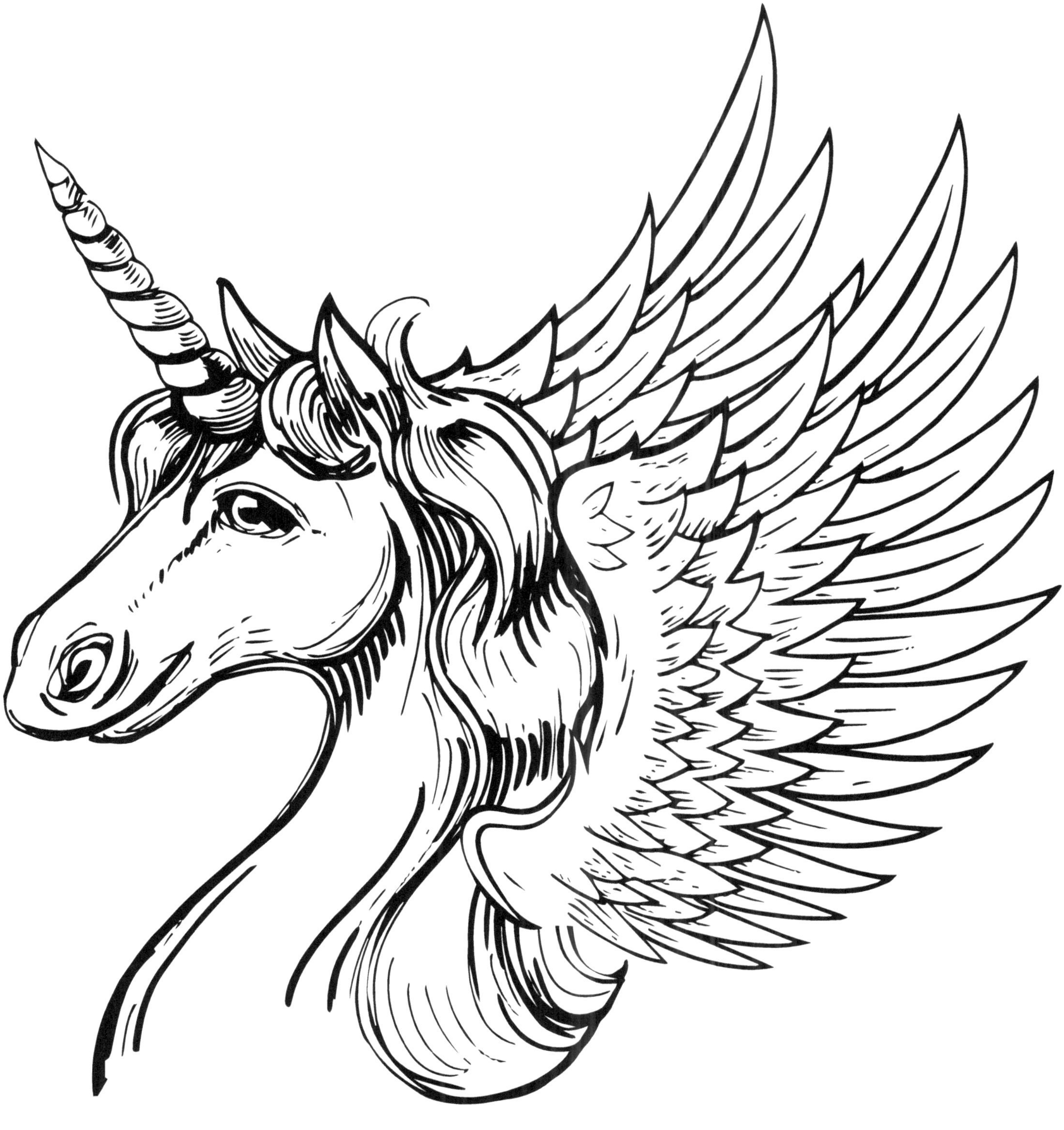

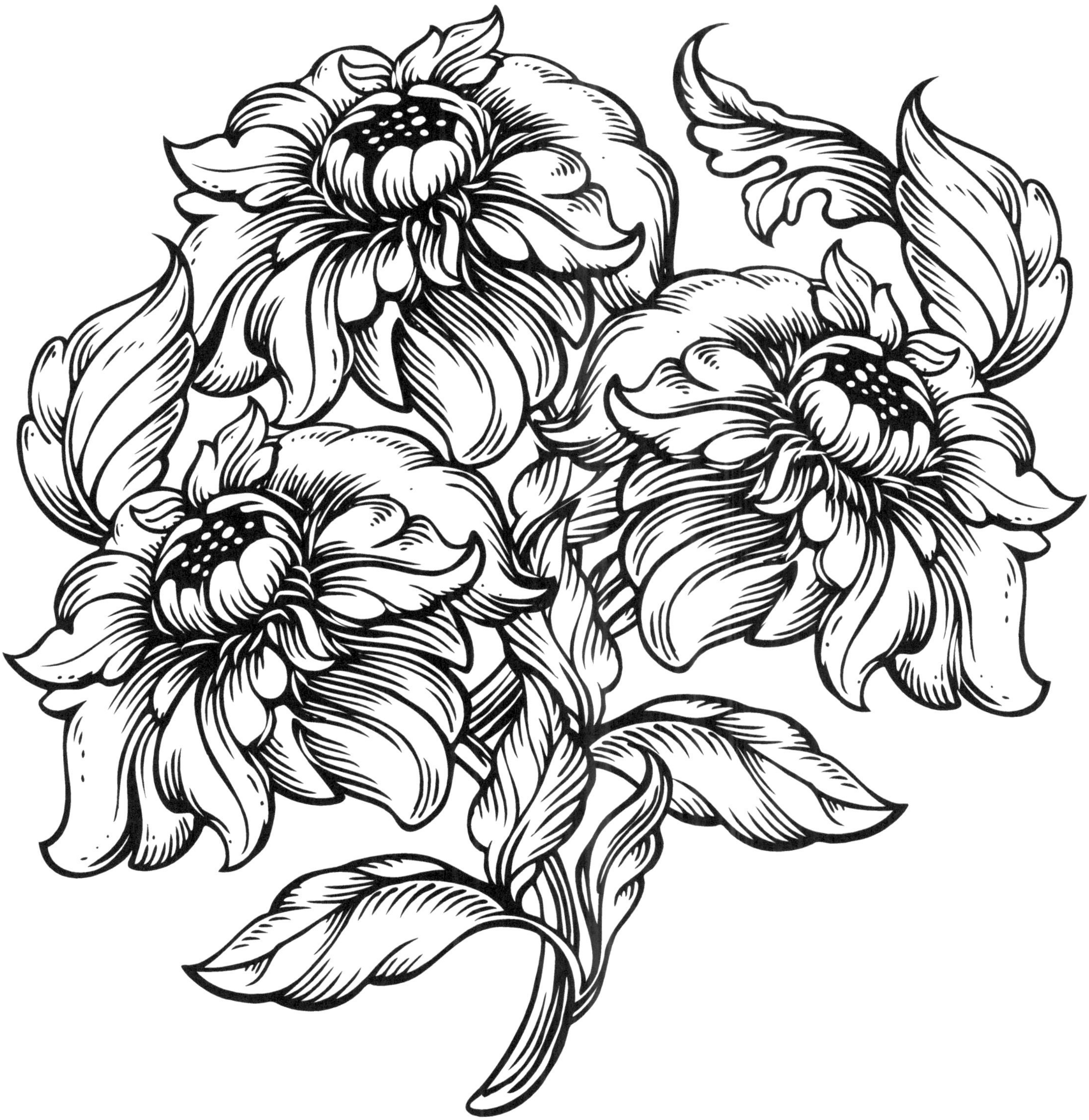

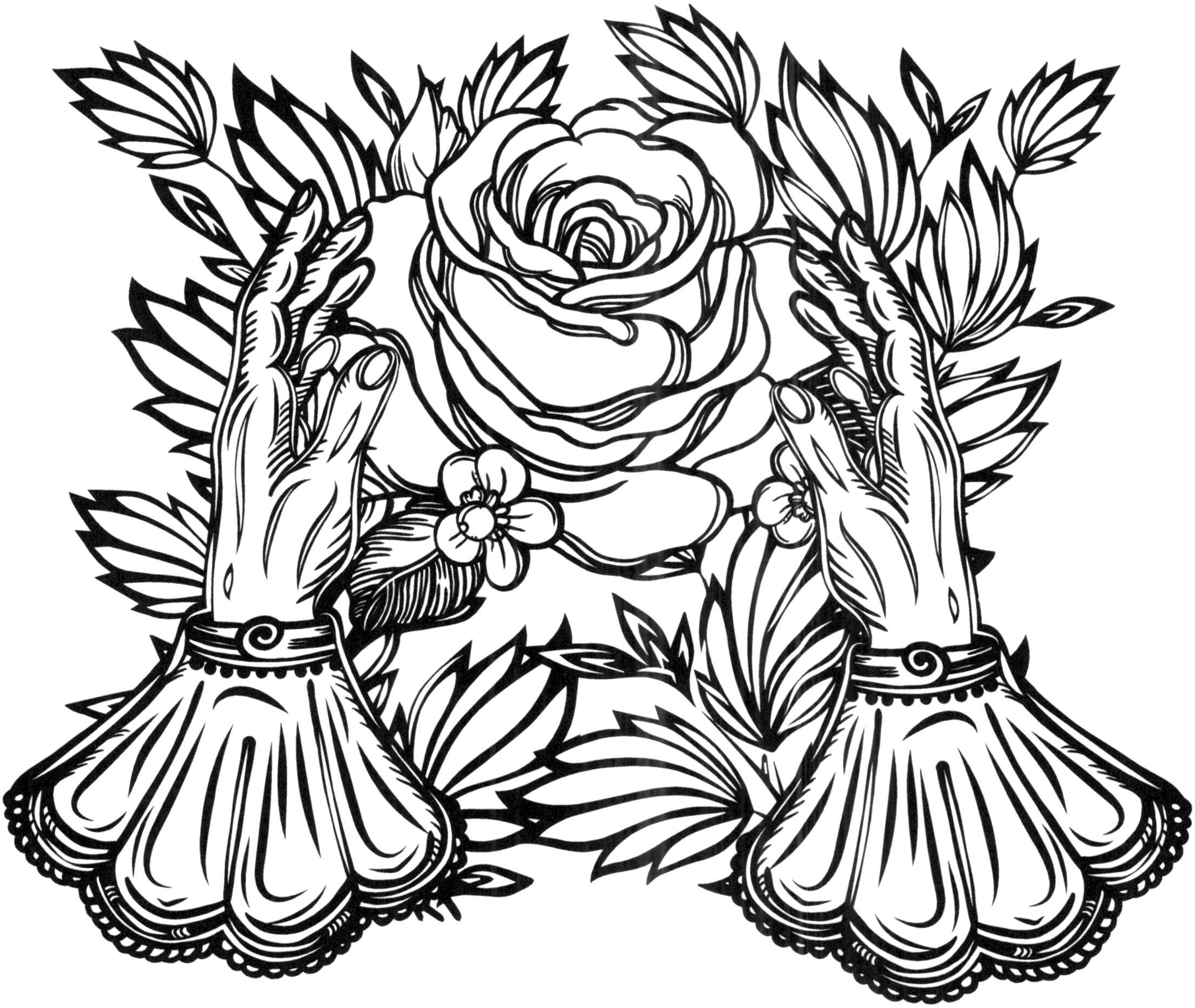

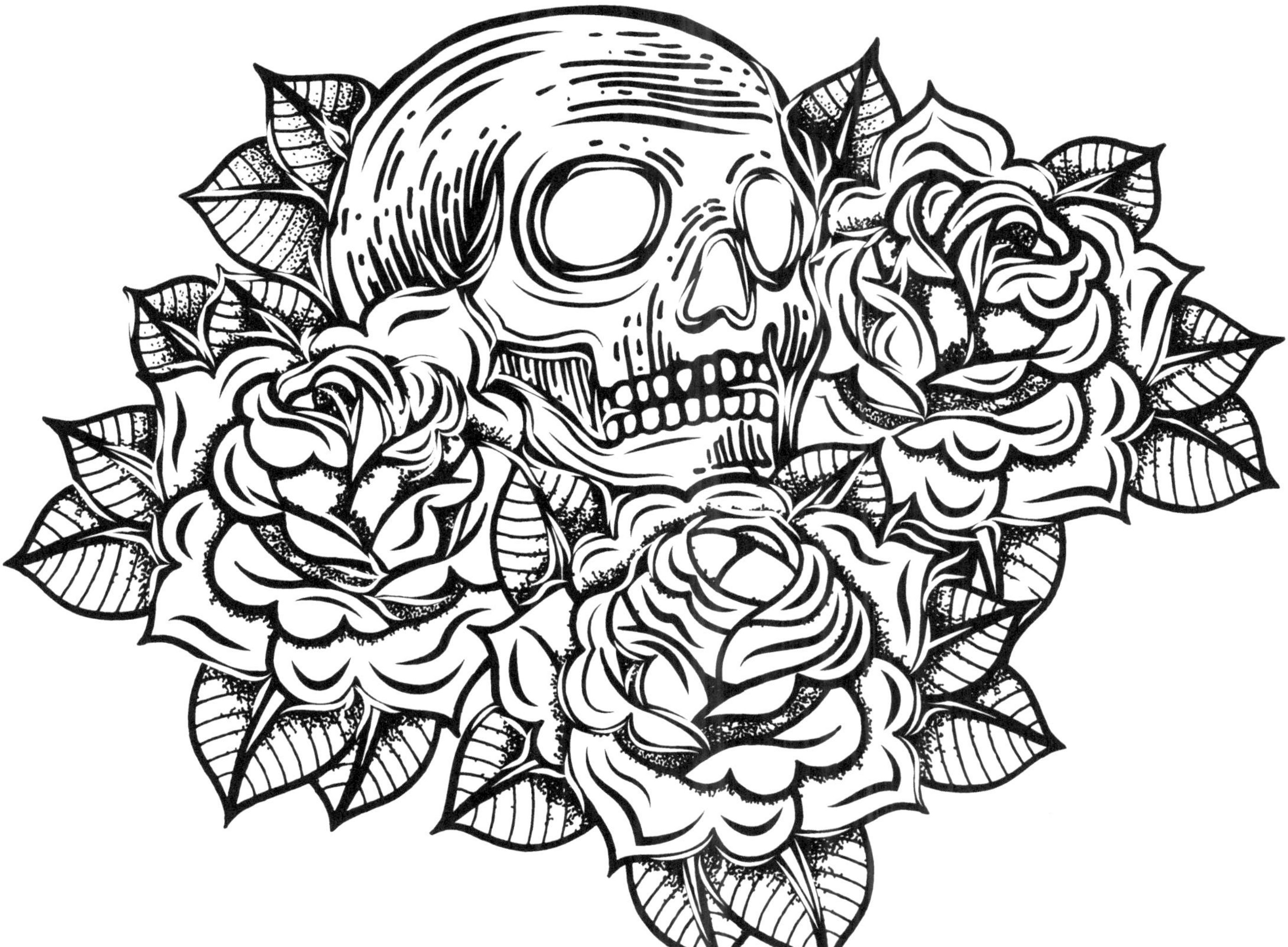

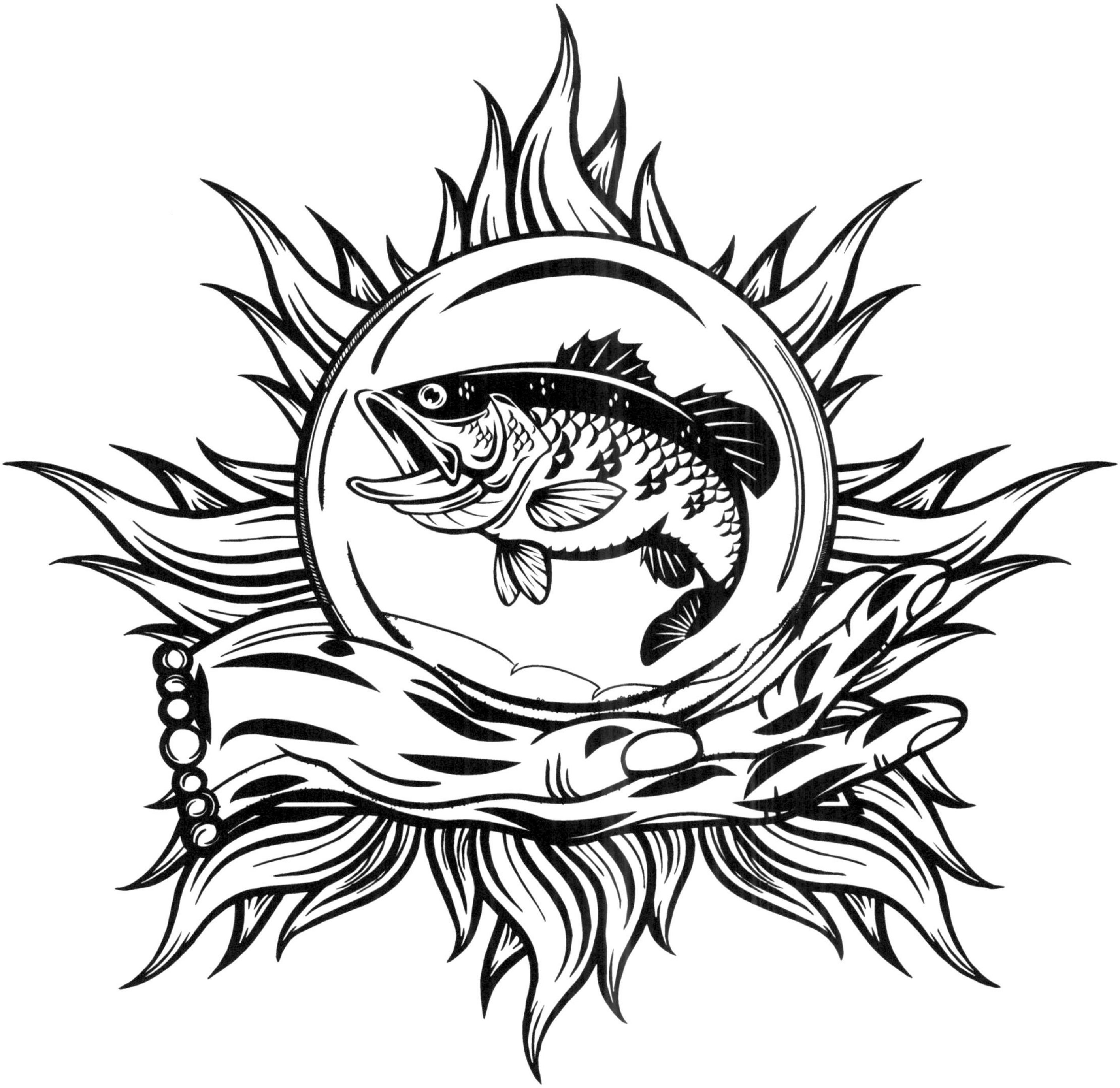

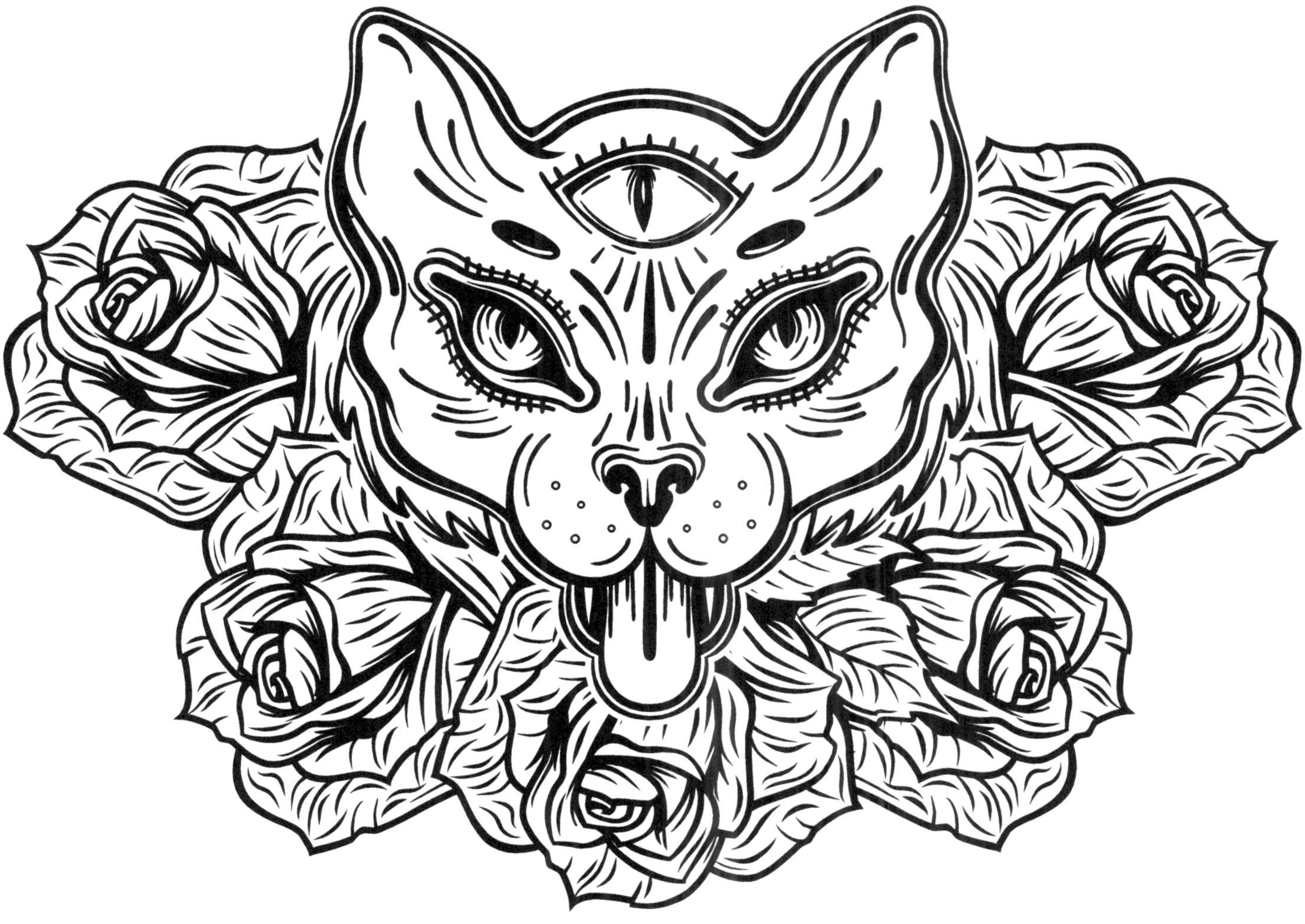

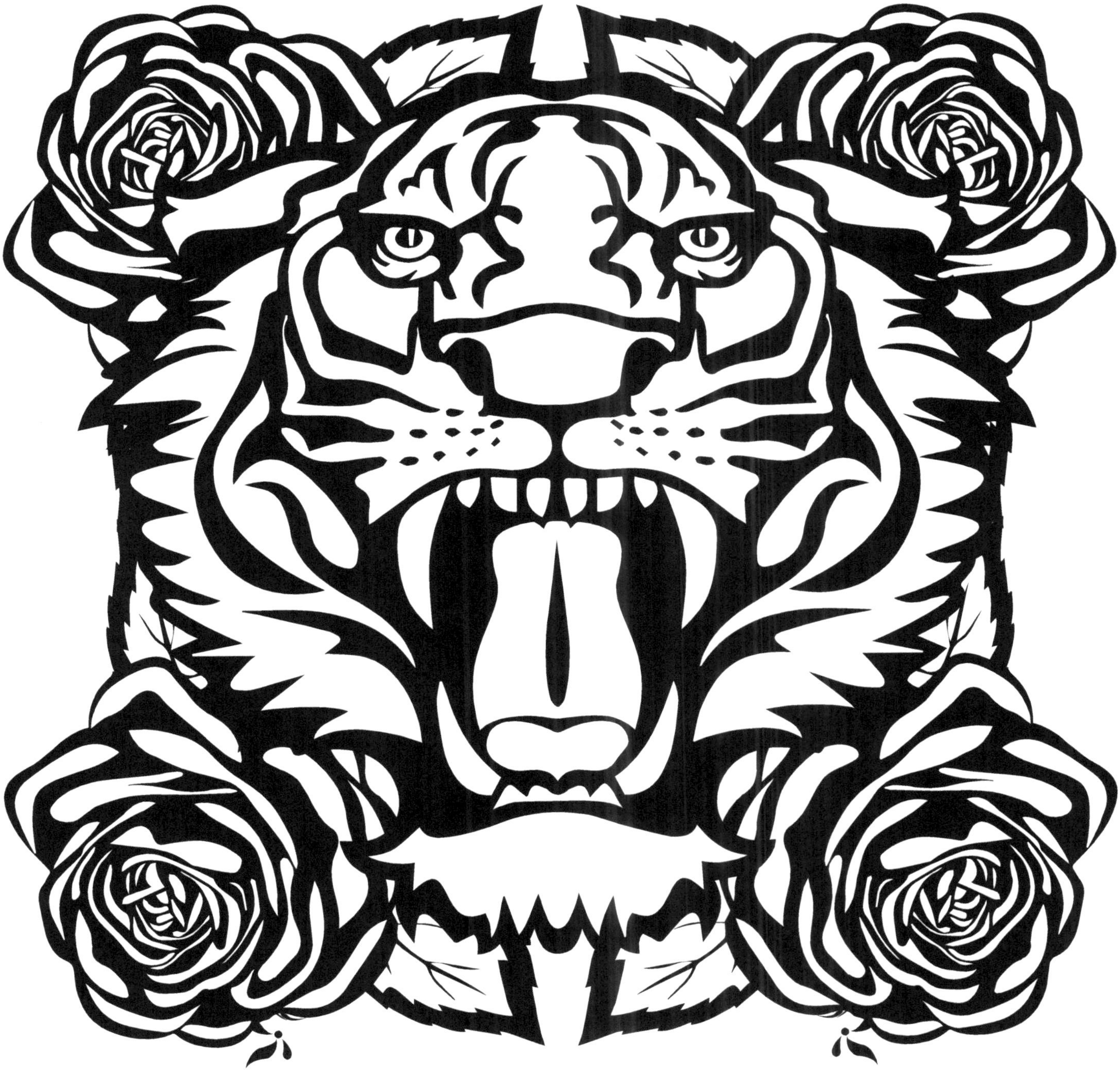

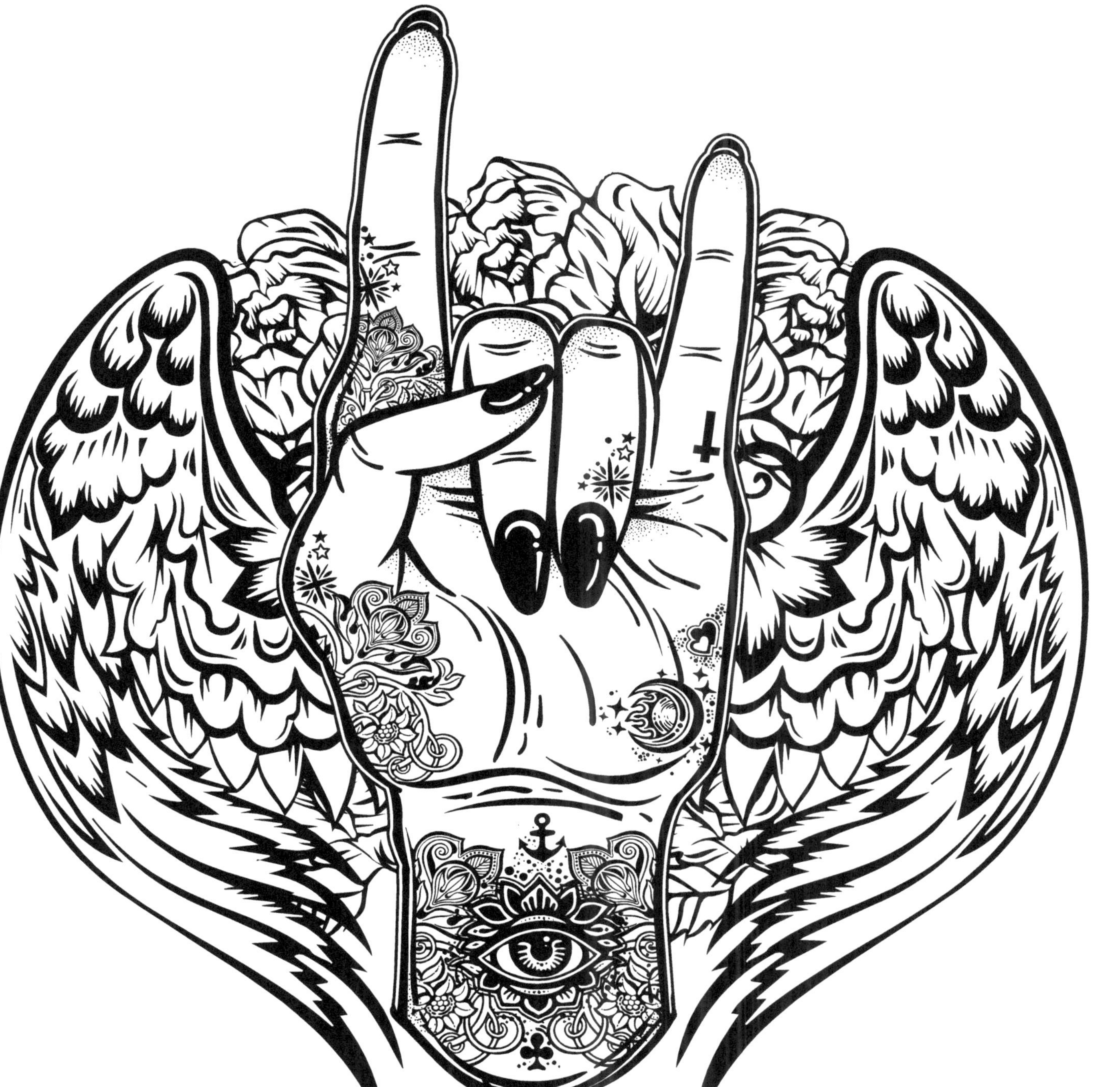

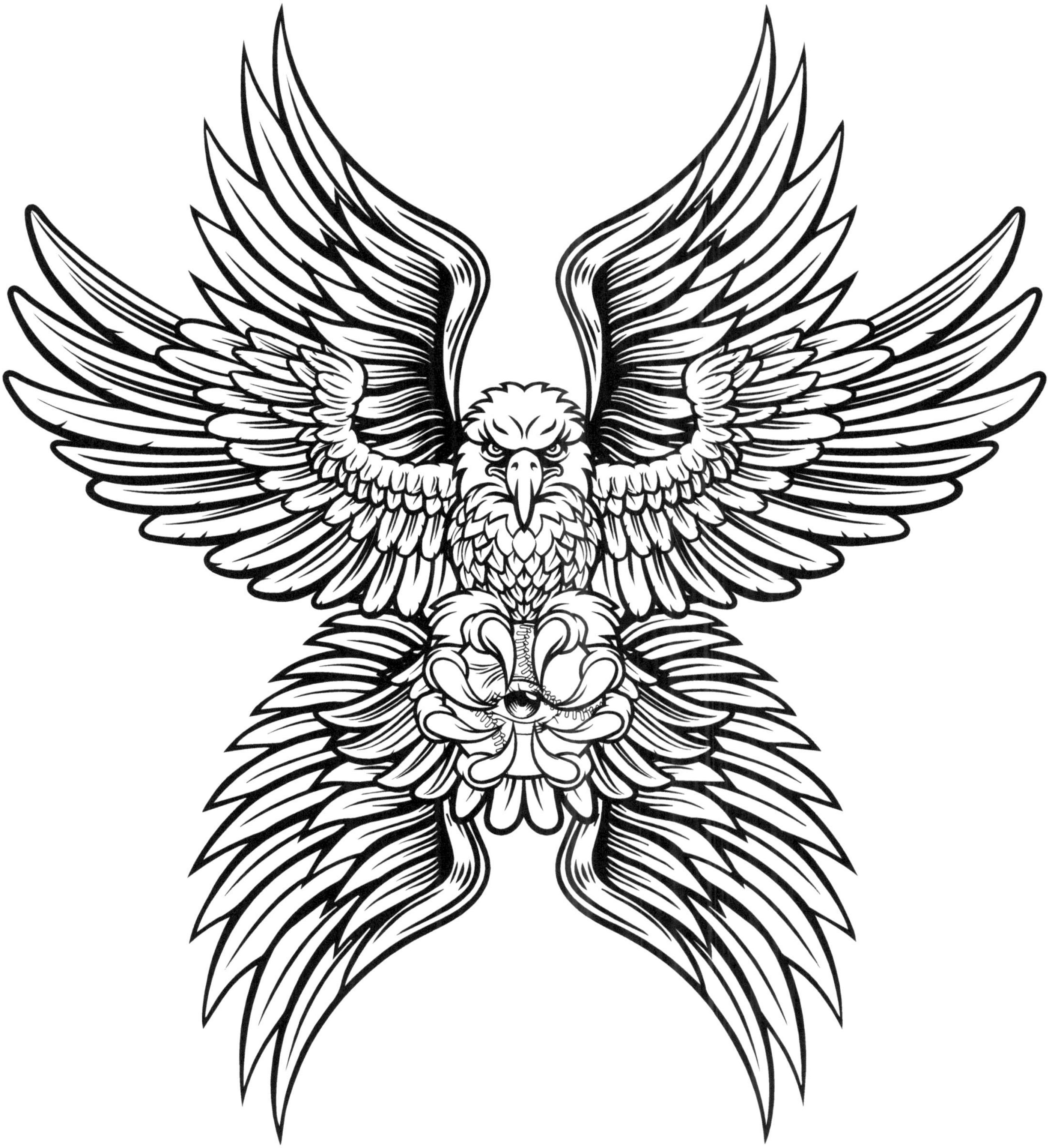

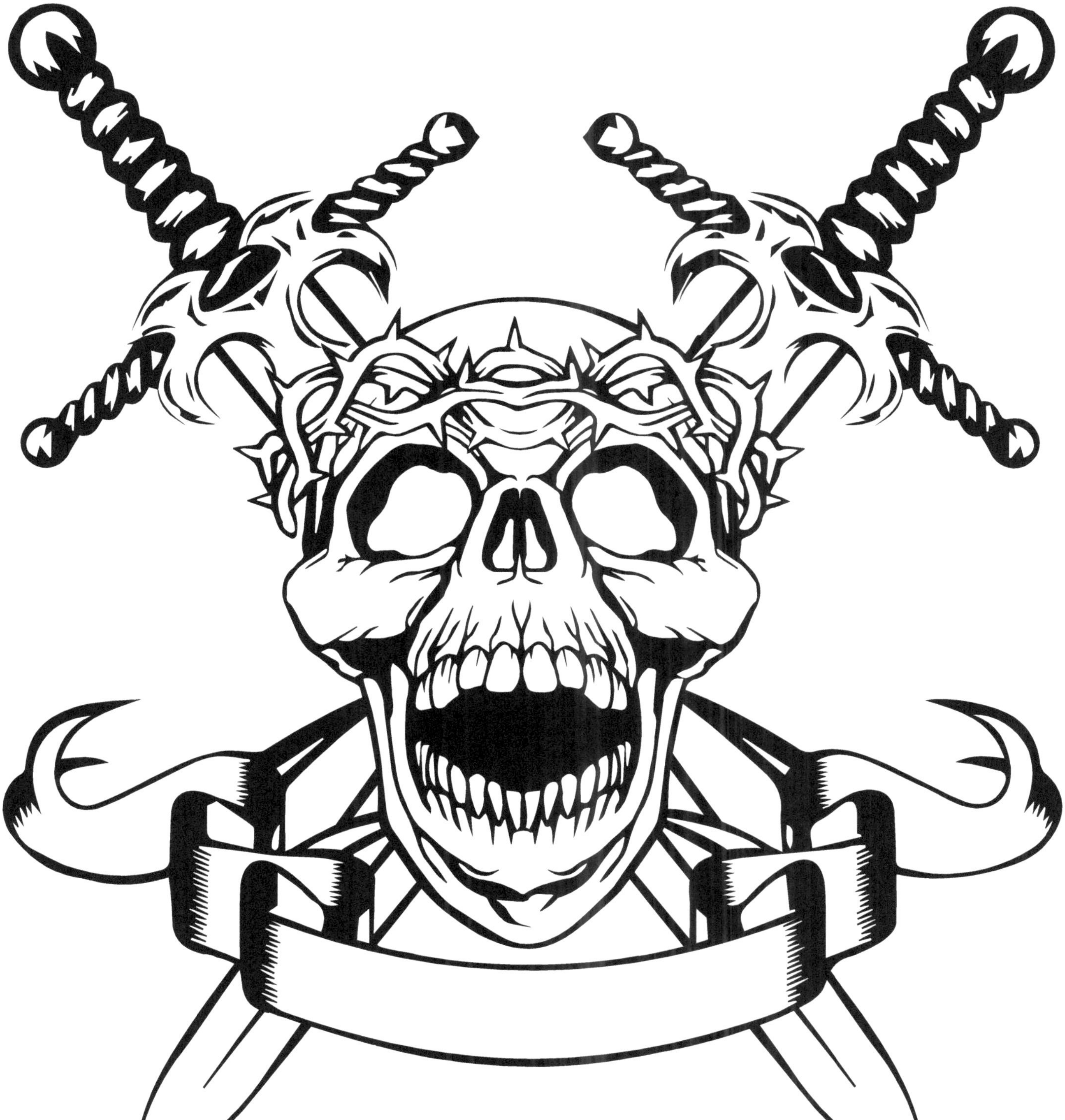

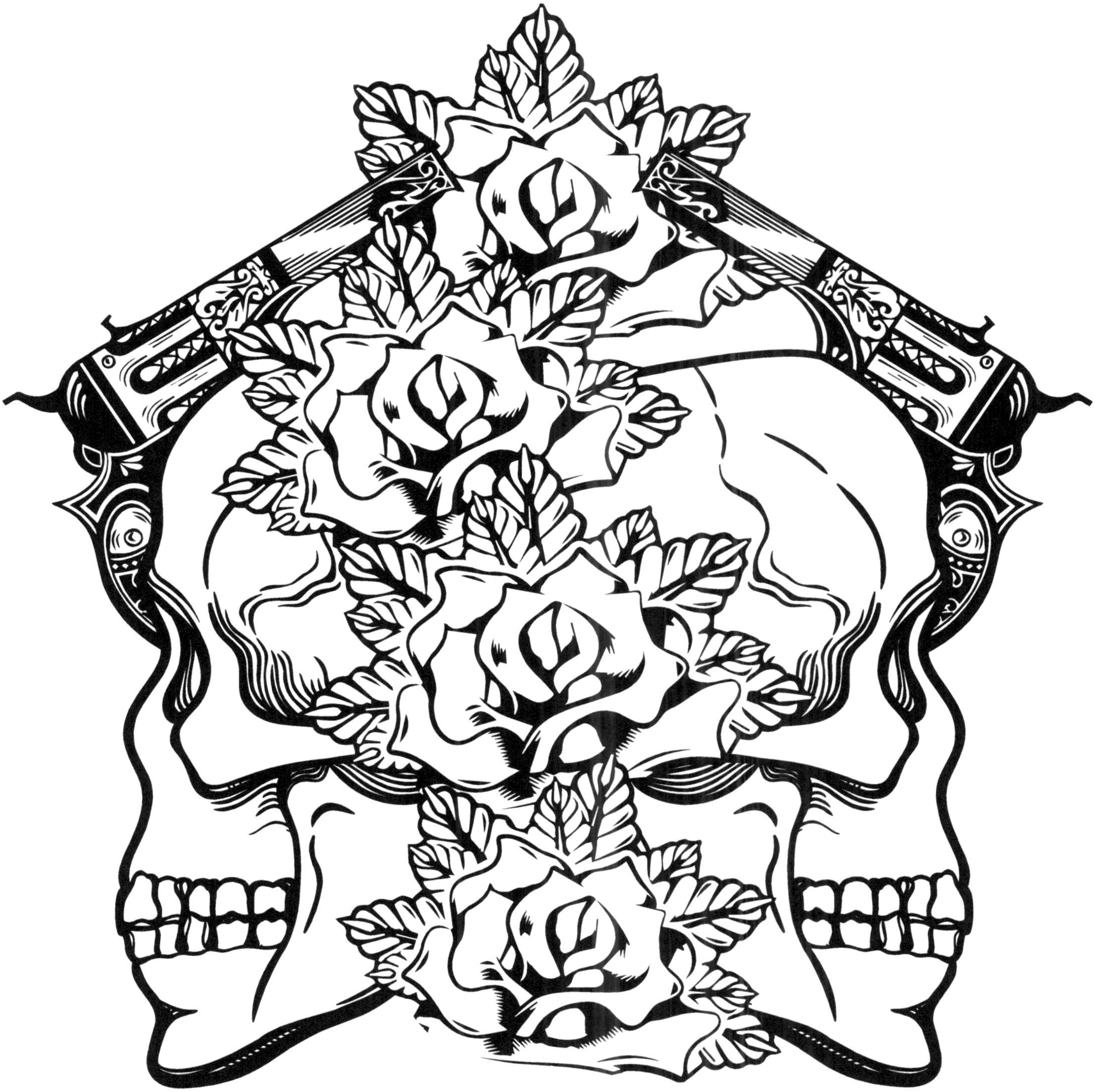

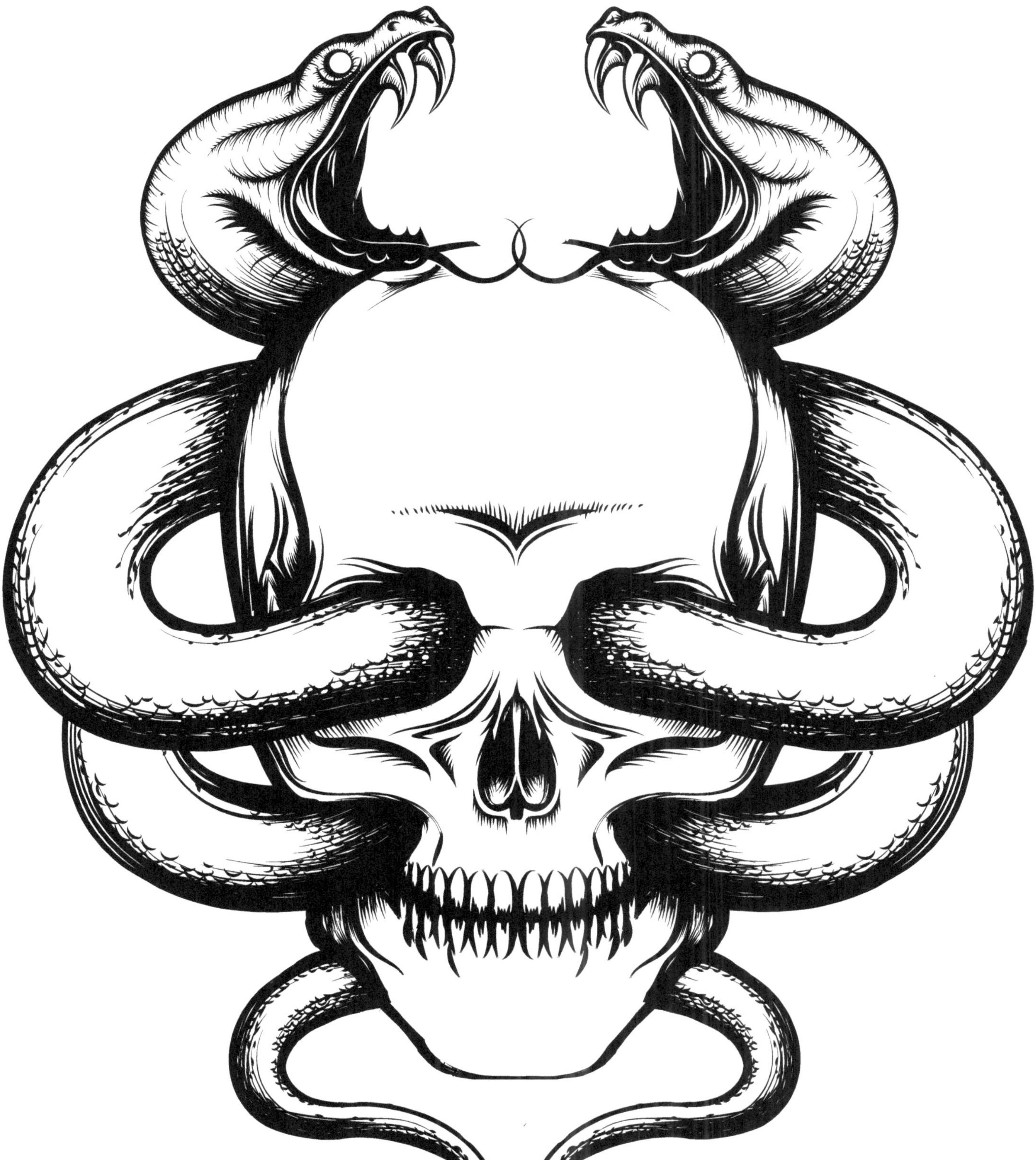

Credit Images to - Katja Gerasimova, Tatiana Apanasova, Marta Leo, Kate Kalita, AlexGreenArt, MorePics,panki, Kudryashka, Julia Waller, John Schwegel, kokitom, Maks TRV, amid999, Christos Georghiou, jatmika jati, Anastasiya Zaplatina, Christopher Brewer, Andrii_M, IMOGI graphics, Bogadeva1983, sunlight 77, Tribalium, VectorPot, Diana Finch, kokitom

Printed in the USA
CPSIA information can be obtained
at www.ICGtesting.com
LVHW080101091124
796116LV00042B/424
9798330402151